T0064728

A Given Choice

A Given Choice

Mary B. Blalock

iUniverse, Inc.
Bloomington

A Given Choice

iUniverse books may be ordered through booksellers or by contacting:

iUniverse
1663 Liberty Drive
Bloomington, IN 47403
www.iuniverse.com
1-800-Authors (1-800-288-4677)

ISBN: 978-1-4759-7402-7 (sc)
ISBN: 978-1-4759-7403-4 (ebk)

Library of Congress Control Number: 2013901856

Printed in the United States of America

iUniverse rev. date: 02/19/2013

In the heat of a moment, "I love you" rolls off the tongue, an expression often lost in translation, void of feeling, and lacking definition. Slipping carelessly past the lips, it is spoken to justify feelings of desire or to heighten erotic pleasure, but sadly, few will ever experience how sweet its taste when communicated from the heart . . . a prelude to love everlasting. And, without that knowledge, one will never know how truly passionate a kiss can be.

MBB

Prelude

Running throughout the valley, a lone dirt road winds for miles, curving its way between the mountainous terrain and rocky ridges of Lando Ferry, and following the trail, a rickety wagon leaves behind a cloud of dust. Poplars and silver birch line either side, their shadows offering sporadic relief from the sun's sweltering rays, their dense foliage a muffle for the rhythmic beat of horses' hooves, while in the branches, a cardinal announces the arrival of springtime.

On a hillside, bent and withered beyond his years, a farmer walks behind a mule-drawn plow, and rushing to his father's side, a child lugs a pail of fresh spring water. Parched from the heat and dust, the man gulps thirstily, paying no regard to the liquid dripping freely from his chin. He fills his palm with cool water and splashes a sunburned face, and pulling a worn handkerchief from his back pocket, he wipes the sweat from his brow, his eyes involuntarily scrolling the field of unturned acreage. Sighing wearily, he returns to the task at hand, his thoughts on supper, his back aching for the easy chair.

A gurgling creek trickles downstream, and on the banks, young boys fidget impatiently, dropping their lines in the shallow water in hopes of catching a string of trout, a tasty change from the usual beans and cornpone.

The houses, few and far between, are of modest form, the adjoining property a duplicate of the first, and the next no different . . . nor the next.

A mere dot on a county map, Lando Ferry nestles at the foot of the Blue Ridge Mountains in Virginia, a raw and open land untouched by progress or greed. It is the early 1900's, an era of growing up too soon and dying too young, a time when girls become mothers barely past puberty, a boy is a man by the age of sixteen, and forty is old. Hard work, respect, and honesty are the golden rules for survival in this land of common existence, and it is only in the hearts of simpletons and mindless souls that frivolity and foolishness find sanction.

Couples enter the bonds of holy matrimony fully cognizant of their obligation, an unwritten agreement constructed of need or convenience, as more often than not, it is a loveless arrangement.

Men learn early on to seek out women willing to cook, clean, and appease their needs at night. They live by the Bible and the seat of their pants, and the women abide by their men's decisions, expecting little more than a roof over their heads and a father for their children.

Only a handful of youngsters attend school or social outings, and as for the others, a hard day in the field is all the learning they will ever need. It prepares them for the kind of life they are destined to follow, an unsympathetic passage in their father's footsteps.

The little ones are in bed by eight o'clock and asleep without further ado, and shortly after, are followed by their parents. Dreams of a game of tag or whoop and hide dance in their heads, while anyone over the age of twelve is, most likely, too tired to dream at all.

They are awakened at five o'clock sharp by the sound of the rooster's crow, and the aroma of freshly brewed coffee is enough to stimulate even the drowsiest sleepyhead. They rise without a complaint, already dressed and prepared for the events of the day before coming to the table for a full breakfast of biscuits and fatback gravy, eggs and jam. All their meals are eaten together, and those who lag behind, do without.

On Sunday morning, everyone gathers at the Baptist church. They come to sing hymns of faith and to catch up on the goings-on among their neighbors. The front pews are crowded with God-fearing, law-abiding Christians, while in the back of the room, a handful of sinners take up the usual space. Scared by their fear of damnation, children sit quietly, and of the few who dare to misbehave, a good thrashing in the woodshed quickly sets them back on the path to righteousness. After two hours from the pastor's sermon on fire and brimstone . . . the ultimate wages of sin . . . they head home for Sunday dinner, and on Monday morning, they relive it all over again.

At a farmstead three miles outside of town limits, Rebecca and her husband are much like their neighbors, down-to-earth, hardworking, and respectable. In spite of the challenges they face daily, the couple has managed to prosper . . . their needs tended, their wants mollified . . . but this has not always been the case for Rebecca. Having grown up in an orphanage, she has learned to expect little from life, to make do with what she has, and to be appreciative of all things.

At forty-four, Rebecca has endured more than her share of ailments, her health damaged by years of undernourishment and lack of medical attention, her heart weakened further by a failed pregnancy, but she hasn't let it deter her from taking on her share of the workload, the never-ending chores which, at times, seem to consume her.

Her days are drawn from the same pattern, and she rises early, greeting each sunrise as the one before. She has breakfast on the table before waking her husband, and along with the usual household chores, she milks the cow, churns butter, and more days than not, labors in the field alongside her husband from the break of dawn into the fading sunset.

On this day, it is mid-afternoon, and an excited Rebecca stands near the mailbox, an envelope clutched tightly in her trembling hand. Through the years, she has received a hundred such letters, a treasury of memories from her past, each tucked safely away in the bottom of her bureau. She holds the letter close to her heart, always pleased to hear from the young man whose childhood, too, has survived the orphanage, and she smiles to herself as she fondly thinks of Teddy, knowing that the contents inside will bring her news from Knoxville. Looking over her shoulder, she tucks the crumpled note inside her brassiere, saving it for later when she can savor every word, but for now, she has errands to do.

Today is her husband's birthday, and needing fresh eggs for the chocolate cake she is planning to bake, she heads to the henhouse. She steps carefully on her way to the barn, pausing a moment to watch him plowing in the field. He waves to her, and with a flip of her hand, she acknowledges him, a tired smile on her face, a shadow of penitence in her eyes.

Her basket filled with eggs, she ascends the sagging rungs to the back entrance, her steps slow, and exhausted, she eases in the porch swing. Again, her attention is drawn to her husband moving steadily through the rows of newly-planted corn and her heart aches at the sight of him, his shoulders stooped from over-exertion, his face determined to finish the field before nightfall. She has more respect for the man she married than any man she's ever known, and together, they have raised a daughter, all grown now and moved away. Not wanting any part of farm life, the girl moved to the city. She writes regular, and Rebecca cherishes those letters, placing them alongside the others she has stowed away.

In the brightness of a mid-day sun, squeaks from a rusty swing soothe her to relaxation, and Rebecca yawns. She never takes naps, never has time to, but lately, she has found herself easily tired and worn to a frazzle. Involuntarily, she closes her eyes, and without meaning to, she drifts off to sleep, her dreams taking her back to another time . . . a time of innocence, a place of unimaginable cruelty, and the boy who changed it all.

Year of 1902

In the year of nineteen hundred and two, Lando Ferry went about business as usual. In the fields, young lads walked the lengthy rows of tobacco alongside their fathers, their faces hot and sticky, their hands dirty from the toil of the land, while back at the house, tubs filled with rainwater came to a boil over an open fire. Up to their elbows in sudsy froth, women labored over washboards, scrubbing diligently to remove grit and grime from heavily soiled clothes, their fingers nicked and bleeding. The older girls tended to their younger siblings, while within their mother's eyesight, newborns slept peacefully beneath the trees, a sheet stretched above their heads to deter flying insects and a padded quilt to soften an uneven pallet of sod and crabgrass.

This is life in Lando Ferry, and in the valley, it is a good life, simple and unassuming, and the only one they know.

While life in the valley presented a front of seemingly tolerant serenity, it offered a camouflage for the ugliness of evil that dwelled behind the trees. Deep in the hollow, hidden away from the rest of the world, a sweet, yet sinister tale unfolded.

Behind the thickets and far away from curious eyes, hearts within the walls of Sweet Haven Orphanage trembled in fear. The custodian, Ms. Ambrose, a hostile woman standing over six feet tall, big boned and coarse, towered over the misfortunate foundlings, her stature alone enough to induce nightmares, and when that failed to gain results, she quickly resorted to her enforcers, a heavy ruler and leather strap. With an iron hand, she dealt the doom of ill-fated babes and runaways, often denying them medical attention, and at times, rationed food and necessities . . . even toilet privileges . . . to keep them in line. Many times, the children were sent to bed without supper or berated with an assault of furious accusations over some minor issue, and when she felt her weapons were not punishment enough, she turned the poor waifs over to Big Bruce, the groundskeeper. He was a giant of a man and ignorant to the ways of the world. Stooped from arthritis, he kept a heavy rod by his side, a constant reminder of Ms. Ambrose's authority and control, and of those who had faced Bruce for disciplinary action, no one ever spoke of his choice of punishment. No one dared.

Rebecca had lived here as long as she could remember, and she knew the ways and rules of the home by heart. Through her own instincts of survival, she had learned to keep her nose clean, staying to herself and creating as little attention as possible. She blended in with the tattered walls and drab furniture, and mostly, was just forgotten. Rarely had she faced the punishment of Ms. Ambrose, and never had she been alone with Big Bruce.

By the age of twelve, Rebecca bore the responsibility of keeping the house clean and supervising the little ones. She prepared meals, made beds, and scrubbed clothes by hand, and being the eldest, not only did she manage the home and children, but tended to the outdoor chores as well, carrying buckets of water from the spring and chopping wood for the cook stove. She did whatever was necessary to make the orphanage a home, and on occasion, had used her skills to trap a rabbit for stew as well as wringing a chicken's neck for a pot of Sunday dumplings.

She took great care to watch over the children, but she could not always stop the sudden rage of Ms. Ambrose. More times than she cared to remember, she had witnessed the onslaught of terror unleashed upon the defenseless babes, and there was nothing she could do except to comfort them when it was over. She rocked them and sang softly until their tears subsided, not knowing how long she would be here for them.

The children looked to the young girl as their guardian angel, and at the close of each day, they quietly gathered at her feet while she filled their minds with tales of a fantasy life far away, of better times and happier days to come.

"There's a world out there that don't know nothing about what goes on in here," she'd say, her country voice ringing with sweet hope. "Someday, I'm going there, and you can too. Out there, won't be nobody tell us nothing that we can't do."

"Can I go with you?" asked Teddy.

Rebecca always responded with the same answer, "Nah, I can't take you with me, baby, but I'll come back for you. Okay? I'll come back and get ever one of you."

"Me too?" asked two-year-old Gracie.

"Especially you," she answered.

"You ever been out there?" asked Michael, a five-year-old girl whose only legacy from her father was his name.

"No, honey, I ain't never been nowhere," Rebecca told her. "But, I heard what it's like. Out there, kids live a whole different life than us. Why, they have ice cream ever day of the week if they want it, and cookies for supper . . ."

"You ever eat ice cream?" inquired Teddy.

"Yeah," she said. "One time when I was about five, these people from the church come to see us and they brung some. There was this one little girl who come with em, and she talk to me some. She say she eats ice cream ever day and twice on Sunday."

"What did it taste like?"

"It taste something like milk, only sweet. They say it was spose to be thick, but it melt afore they got here. But, us younguns didn't care. It was still good."

"What else did that girl tell you?"

"She told me so much stuff my head ain't big enough to keep it all. What I remember best is how she say everday is just like Christmas . . ."

"Christmas?"

"Christmas is when kids get to make a wish for something they want, and if they been good, they get it, and if they been bad, then all they get is switches."

"Then we must be awful bad," pondered Bobby, his voice sad, his face downcast.

"No, baby!" Rebecca rushed to explain. "We ain't bad! We special, that's all! We don't get our wishes cause we already got the best thing in the world! We got each other, and that's way better'n some old ball or spin-top!"

Not wanting to miss a thing, Teddy sat on the edge of his chair absorbing every word. He had heard the story before, as they all had, but somehow, each telling spun them in a new direction, often ending with a different conclusion. He urged her to continue. "Tell us some more stuff. Tell what it's like when it gets cold outside."

"Well, when it gets cold outside and the wind blows hard, you won't even know it!" Rebecca said, her eyes wide. "And you know why? Cause you be snug as a bug, that's why! There'll be a fire burning in the hearth, and warm blankets, too . . . enough blankets for everbody . . . and when you lay your head down to sleep, there won't be no more nightmares neither . . . no, unt-huh . . . nary a one! There'll just be dreams of a berry patch, and your bucket's running over with sweet berries . . ."

"What kind of berries?"

"Blackberries and blueberries! Any kind you like! And should you get lost in the woods while you picking em, why it ain't nothing to cause alarm! And you know why? Cause all the animals is your friend, that's why! They'll come up to you and eat right out of your hand."

"But, not the dragons!" Teddy whispered. "Tell about the dragons and the ponies with wings!"

"Oh, yeah, the ponies with wings . . ." Rebecca nodded. "Well, it goes like this . . . poor kids is special kids and they need special attention. That's why God give ever one of em a pony with wings to watch over em. Well, the way it was told to me, way back yonder . . . way afore I was even thought about . . . giant dragons walked all over the land, all bossy-like and making claim to anything they wanted. All summer long, they stomped up and down the mountain doing anything they please, but when winter come, they didn't like the cold one bit, and so they holed up in a cave to wait for spring to come and the snow to melt. Now, all them months of putting up with each other and not having nothing to eat made em even more cantankerous than they was afore, and with their stomachs growling, they come out of the cave awful hungry, mad at everthing, and meaner'n . . . meaner'n . . ."

"Meaner'n Ms. Ambrose!" blurted Gracie.

Rebecca nodded. "Well, these old, mean, hungry dragons start right away looking for little girls to fill their bellies . . ."

"Why just little g-girls?" asked Joe.

"Cause girls taste like a peppermint stick," Michael answered, looking to Rebecca for affirmation.

"That's right," Rebecca agreed. "Just like peppermint. Now, the little boys know these mean old dragons don't want to eat them . . . all acause they taste like three-day-old pollywogs . . . so the boys step up and commence to throwing rocks and sticks at the dragons. They throw anything they can get their hands on to keep em away from the little girls . . . and it's all acause of how the boys stepped up to fight the dragons that got folks to thinking that boys is tougher'n girls, but as you can see, that ain't the case. It's just cause little boys taste so bad . . ."

"How bad?" asked Bobby, not wanting to miss a single detail.

"So bad they could make a buzzard puke! That's why the dragons don't want none of em! Why, it would take a week, maybe a month, to get that nasty taste out of their mouths! Ugh!" Rebecca said, making a face.

While Teddy, Bobby, and Joe giggled at Rebecca's efforts to make them laugh, Butch sat quietly, seeming to take no interest. Smiling at him, she tweaked his nose and continued with the outlandish yarn. "Well, now, the boys keep on throwing rocks and stuff, and after a while, they run out of things to throw, and that's when the dragons make their move. Just when the biggest of the bunch is about to grab one of the little girls . . ."

"Down come the ponies with wings!" Bobby whispered loudly.

"I knowed it!" Teddy exclaimed. "It happens ever time!"

"Shh!" Rebecca warned. "We don't want to rile Ms. Ambrose, do we?"

All the children covered their mouths with their hands, and Rebecca went on, "And when the ponies with wings come down, all the poor boys and girls climbed on their own special pony, and the pony flapped his wings and off they went in the sky."

"Did you ever see one of them ponies?"

"Not in real life," Rebecca answered. "By the time I was born, there wouldn't no more of em left, but I seen one in a book. He was real purty, too! He just had one horn and it was right smack-dab in the middle of his head. But, it wouldn't no ugly horn like the kind a cow has, or like a goat. It was pearly white, and his whole body was covered in purty colors . . . like ever color of a rainbow . . . and his wings was so big they spread all the way from here to yonder!"

Awed by her knowledge, they all agreed, "You shore know a lot of stuff!"

"Yeah, I guess. Someday, you be smart, too, if you pay attention to what folks say. You can learn a lot just by listening to other people. Out there, kids got a school where they can learn and they get most of their learning from books. They be real smart, too . . ."

"How smart?"

"Smarter'n me in some ways. Why, sometimes, they be smarter'n their own mamas and daddies! But, you got to remember one thing, head smarts and book smarts ain't the same thing, but if you use your noggin, it'll get you further than books."

"How's that?" asked Teddy.

"Well, none of us here can read, so how's a book gonna help us?" she explained with logic. "But we all got noggins."

"We all got noggins! We all got noggins!" Teddy mimicked, and to prove his point, he banged his head against the wall.

"Stop that," Rebecca scolded. "If you keep doing that, you gonna rattle your brains and then they won't be no good for nothing. When I say use your head, I mean for something other than butting walls."

"Are you just saying that?" asked Bobby. "About us getting out of here?"

"Course not! You won't always be a little kid, and when you get big, you can leave this place and ain't nobody can stop you. When you all growed up, you can get anything you want if you want it bad enough. And, that's the truth!"

"Me love you, Becca," Gracie said.

"Yeah, I know you do, and I love you too, baby," Rebecca replied, thinking of the lie she had told. But, she reckoned, if it was a lie to give hope to those who had none, then it really wasn't so bad, and maybe God would overlook it this time.

"Come here, baby. Come, and I rock you to sleep."

Gracie climbed on her lap, and Rebecca sang softly, "Rock a bye, baby, in the treetop . . . when the wind blows . . ."

Year of 1905

The early signs of spring were in the air, and Rebecca stood on the porch, her chin propped on the broom in her hand, her mind in a daydream. She studied her image in the windowpane, pale and delicate, her dress hanging loosely over a shapeless frame, and she frowned her disappointment. The portrayal was not that of a young girl approaching womanhood, but a reflection that could easily be mistaken for one of the children. She would be fifteen in another month, and often fantasized herself dressed in polished attire, a handsome woman of finery and poise, but looking at her likeness in the glass, she knew that dream would be a long time coming. She pondered the changes her future might hold, or if *this* was her future . . . this house of misery, hunger, and loneliness.

Interrupting her thoughts, a child's screams tore through the open door, and dropping her broom, she ran inside.

Gracie cringed before her fate, and the spilled water and broken glass on the floor told Rebecca the rest of the story. She stopped short of rushing in and stripping Ms. Ambrose of the dreaded ruler.

"Oh, please, ma'am, I beg you not!" Rebecca pleaded above Gracie's screams, but the ruler came down hard a second time across the top of her tiny fingers.

Ms. Ambrose raised the ruler again, and the other children sought safety behind Rebecca's skirt.

Swallowing hard, Rebecca tried again. "Please, ma'am, I clean it up! Please don't hit her . . ."

"Don't you hit her again, you bat!" came a young male voice from the doorway. "Don't you lay another hand on her!"

Quickly, he strode across the floor, and snatching the ruler from Ms. Ambrose's hand, he broke it across his knee with a loud splintering sound.

Rebecca quickly pulled Gracie out of danger.

"Just what the hell's going on here?" the young man demanded. "What kind of place is this that you can just beat up on a baby? Don't you have a decent ounce in you? Where's Ambrose?"

Ms. Ambrose stood speechless. Never had anyone defied her or questioned her methods of punishment. She looked wildly around the room, daring anyone to take this incident lightly.

Her eyes flashing and teeth clenched tight, she snarled, "I'm Miz Ambrose. Who let you in here, boy? Who are you?"

He answered without flinching. "Name's Crip."

"Well, whoever you are, you can just find your way back out like you find your way in," she barked. "You got no business poking your nose in here."

"I was told to come," he said, waving an envelope. "I got papers that say I'm to work for board . . . it's all right here in this letter."

Ms. Ambrose eyed him with contempt, and the onlookers scarcely breathed as they watched, wide-eyed, to see what would happen next. Merely glancing at the document in her hand, the old woman stomped to the cook stove and tossed the papers in the fire.

"You wait here!" she ordered, and spinning on her heel, she left the room.

The children had never seen anyone like the young man who stood before them, and they huddled together, whispering in awe of the heroic lad whose very presence brought them a sense of safety.

He was of medium build, a little too thin, and he walked with a slight limp. His pants, frazzled and baggy, were cuffed to the tops of his shoes, and buttoned at the throat, a heavily stained duster hung loosely across his arms. Pushed neatly behind the ears, his hair fell just below the shoulders, while light brown wisps escaped the brim of a fedora to fall across his forehead, masking his hardened blue eyes. Unperturbed, he chewed on a stick of birch, his chin protruding with defiance, yet there was a softness in his manner, and Rebecca could not take her eyes off him.

In unison, they watched his every move as he paced around the room, his confidence overwhelming, his bravery implausible. Fearlessly, he had stood up to their evil caretaker, and they all wondered what powers he possessed beneath his common stature, a boy of apparent little means and brawn.

He appeared intrigued by his surroundings, and with an impressive, "Umm," he placed a finger to his chin and nodded, all the while, keeping one eye on his admirers. Amused by their timidity, he suddenly whirled around and whispered loudly, "Boo!"

Startled, they jumped back, and Rebecca frowned disapprovingly. "Who are you?" she asked. "Are you a wizard?"

"Are you a fairy?"

"Becca ain't no fairy," Gracie sniffled, rubbing her eyes with her fists, the ugly red welts still visible and starting to bruise. "She's Becca."

"And, who might you be, little'n?" he asked softly, kneeling on the floor in front of the five-year-old.

"Gracie. Are you a angel?"

"Not hardly. But, I be your angel if you want me to," he told her, rising to his feet and ruffling her hair. With a devilish grin, he leaned close to Rebecca, and lowering his voice, he whispered, "And, I be your angel, too, if you like."

"I don't need no angels to look out for me!" she declared. "You just remember that!"

"A real little spit-fire, ain't you? Well, if you so big and all, then how about you be my angel? I ain't got no problem with a purty girl got red hair and wings setting on my shoulder."

Rebecca had never been in the presence of a young man her own age, her experiences with the opposite sex consisting of young lads and old men, and her face flushed under his gaze. She wanted to come back with something clever to say, but he had called her pretty, and beyond that, her brain refused to function.

She swallowed hard a couple of times, breathing a sigh of relief when eight-year-old Teddy stepped forward to pick up the slack. "What's your name?" he asked.

"It's Crip. You got something to say about that?"

Rebecca tossed her head, rallying to Teddy's defense. "He means, what's your *real* name."

"It's Crip. You deef or something?"

"That ain't no kind of name," she stated with certainty.

"It must be some kind," he said matter-of-factly, "cause it's the kind my mama give me. I was born with this here bum leg, and that's how I got my name. And anyways, it don't sound no worse'n Becca. Where'd you get that name?"

"It's Rebecca to you, and I don't know how I got the name being as I never had a mama, so . . ."

"Never had a mama? Why, everbody's *had* a mama. How else do you think you got here?"

"For all you know, maybe I come from an egg," she told him. "Maybe all of us did."

Bobby inched forward, his twin brother, Joe, following cautiously behind. "Are you going to stay here with us?"

"If I like it, I will," he said. "And if I don't, then I won't."

"Like it?" Rebecca scoffed. "Ain't that a laugh! If you got your sights set on liking it here, ain't no need hanging your hat on no nail cause I spect you be gone first thing in the morning!"

"That's what you spect? Well, I spect I might stick around for a little while," he said, his eyes roaming the room. "And, then again, I might not. It just depends."

"You ain't old enough to be saying when you can come and go," she challenged. "How old are you, anyways?"

"Old enough to eat cornpone without getting choked," he replied.

"Any three-year-old could do the same, so that don't say much."

"If you have to know, I'm fourteen . . . fifteen soon enough. How old are you?"

"Old enough to know a liar when I hear one," she grinned, beginning to enjoy the joshing. "You ain't a day over thirteen . . . if that."

"If you know so much, what'd you ask me for? I'm fourteen, same as fifteen! It's just that this here busted leg makes me seem like I ain't growed up, yet."

"Is that a fact? All I see is a scrawny kid trying to fit a big man's britches! That's all I see . . . strutting in here like you know stuff. Old Ambrose will set you straight afore tomorrow's done. That is, if you last that long."

"And, you think I'm going to let anything you say carry weight?" he asked, tugging at her ponytail. "I mean, you coming from an egg and all."

"Well, I bet you don't stay here," she said, slapping his hand away. "Ain't nobody got a right mind if they do."

He stood in front of her, so close she could feel his breath on her cheek, his eyes penetrating. Her heart raced, and for a moment, she was almost afraid he was going to kiss her. For a fleeting second, she almost wished he would. After all, he *had* said she was pretty.

He moistened his lips. "So, that's what you think? That I'd have to be crazy to stay here?"

With a heavy sigh, her spunk waned, and she answered, her voice as desolate as the hollowness in her eyes, "Ain't nothing to think about. It's just the way it is."

Gracie tugged at his arm. "Don't go! I want you to stay!"

Crip patted the top of her head. "I ain't going nowhere, little'n. At least, not today."

"Where'd you come from?" asked Michael.

"Here and there. I been around."

"Around where?"

"All over," he said, gesturing with an air of importance.

His cockiness spurred Rebecca to wipe the smug look off his face. "All over?" she jeered. "I ain't never heard of a place called *all over*."

"Well," he drawled, studying her, "that don't mean nothing just cause you ain't never heard of it. I spect there's a lot of places you ain't never heard of."

"What's that spose to mean? You think I'm dumb?"

"No, I wouldn't say dumb. Ignorant, maybe."

"Well, you know what I think?" she retorted. "I think you just talk bull about a lot of stuff, but don't really know squat about nothing!"

He tilted his head to one side, and under his stare, she blushed a deep shade of red. With a twinkle in his eye, he pulled the twig from his mouth and lightly touched it to her lips, thoroughly enjoying her discomfort. "If I recall it right," he grinned broadly, "I don't remember asking what *you* think."

The door swung open, and a hush fell across the room when Ms. Ambrose stepped inside.

"Go get your details from Bruce. Make shore that you listen and learn what I spect out of you! The way you bust up in here, that ain't the way things are done. I'm in charge of this place, and we have rules," she told him, pointing to the children. "They keep em, and they won't be broke by the likes of you."

When the door closed behind him, Gracie covered her mouth with her hand. "Is he coming back?" she whispered.

Rebecca stared after him, her face flushed.

Gracie tugged at her skirt. "Is he coming back?" she repeated.

"Yeah, baby," Rebecca answered absently. "He be back."

"How you know?" asked Teddy.

"He say he ain't going nowhere . . . not today."

"But, you say he's a liar!" Bobby reminded her.

"Oh, he's a liar, alright. But, he be back. Just like he say."

Days turned into weeks and weeks into months as spring slowly progressed into summer. Crip had seen fit to remain at Sweet Haven . . . at least until something better came along, he said . . . and had proved himself a worthy hand, toiling the field of rocks and weeds to make a bountiful garden. From sunup to sundown, he worked long hours, and at night, Rebecca could hear him moving about restlessly in his room next to hers.

The young man had quickly become their hero, and experiencing their first months of freedom and calmness, the children emerged from their shells to share their hopes, opinions, and ideas.

Having had some learning, he began to teach Rebecca to read, spell, and work with numbers. Many nights after the others had gone to bed, they pored over the books . . . heads close, hands brushing . . . and at first, she had felt uneasy to be in such close contact with a boy who, by his own admission, had declared her pretty.

But, months had passed, and she now had reservations that his words held one ounce of truth, for he had not spoken of it again, and if not for the burn in her cheeks every time it crossed her mind, she would doubt her own recollection of the incident as well. They had settled into an amiable relationship, and although he continued to tease her unmercifully, she had come to expect the raillery, even to enjoy it.

He was wonderful with the children, playing games and telling stories, and they rushed to get their chores done, eager to be part of his next venture. His coming had brought them a taste of stability and contentment, and they ran about as children do, laughing for no other reason than they liked the sound of it.

The creek beyond the trees became their private gathering place, and they arranged meetings with whispers passed along from one to the other. They came here as often as they could get away, sometimes only for a few minutes, but it was enough to give them a sense of acceptance and belonging. At Sweet Haven, they were an assembly of orphans, but at the creek, they were a family.

The middle of July was hot and humid, and Crip summoned a meeting.

"Why we come here?" asked Michael. "What's it all about?"

"Ain't about nothing but cooling off," Crip told her. "I was sweating like a preacher in a whore house and this creek kept calling my name."

"What did the creek say?" asked Gracie, her eyes big.

"It said, *Crip, you go get them little younguns and take em swimming!*"

Gracie giggled, and Rebecca scowled. "What you must be thinking? The sun ain't even got high in the sky yet, and it's too early to be sneaking off down here. We going to get in trouble if the old lady finds out."

"And, who's going to run and tell?" he asked. "You, Angel?"

"You know I ain't! But, she's got ways of figuring out stuff."

"Don't take more'n five minutes to cool off, and you already waste four of em with your hemming and hawing. Now, get your clothes off . . . all of you . . . and hang em on that bush over there so they don't get wet."

Rebecca blushed profusely at his suggestion, her eyes wide and mouth open, and protectively, she folded her arms across her chest.

"Aw, go on!" he nudged her. "You ain't got nothing nobody wants to look at!"

Blushing, she retorted, "And, how would you know that, mister? You don't know what I got!"

She stepped behind a tree to undress, and neatly folding the gingham pinafore, she draped it over a limb. She didn't care whether anybody wanted to see what she had or not, she was *not* going to remove her bloomers and camisole!

"Turn your head!" she called, peeping from the shrubbery, and guardedly, she stepped into the open, hugging her garments tightly against her body.

On impulse, Crip turned around, grinning broadly. "What did I tell you, skinny angel? Nothing!"

She slapped at him, quickly pulling her hand back to cover the small mounds barely hinting at the promise of evolving breasts.

"I say to turn your head!" she fussed.

With a disinterested look, he slipped out of his jeans. "What's all the fuss?" he asked defensively. "I did just like you say. I turned my head . . ." and, roaring with laughter, he blustered, "turned my head to look at you!"

She drew back as if to slap him again, but he jumped out of her reach and made a dash for the water.

It was not unusual for the young boys and girls to swim in the nude, as they often took baths together, but the early signs of pubertal changes were an awkward reminder of their striking differences, and Rebecca and Crip swam in their underwear, keeping a respectable distance between them.

Watching the children splash about, Butch sat quietly on the creek bank, his feet in the water.

"Get in!" Rebecca invited, splattering a handful of water at him.

Shyly, he shook his head, content to watch.

Rebecca had seen dozens of children come and go, but none had tugged at her heartstrings more than Butch. He had seen more in his nine years than most people see in a lifetime, left alone night after night while his parents had hit the taverns. Coming home intoxicated, they fought with each other, often teaming up to take their frustrations out on him. One night while liquored up, his father shot his mother to death, and when the sheriff arrived on the scene, his dad turned the gun on himself. Butch had been a witness to it all.

He was a pitiful, doleful child, neglected and near starvation when he came to Sweet Haven, and after three years, he still refused to interact with the other children, speaking only when directly spoken to, and even then, he would not lift his eyes from the floor. A frail, lonely lad with hopeless eyes, his health had improved little since coming to the orphanage, standing head to head with Gracie and tipping the scales shy of fifty pounds.

Splashing about in the water, they forgot the time, and the morning slipped by without notice.

"Shh!"

"You younguns better get here right now!" Ms. Ambrose's screech resounded through the treetops.

While the children scrambled for their clothes, Rebecca lingered in the water.

"You better come on!" Crip coaxed, pulling his shirt over his head.

"Hand me my dress!" she hissed.

"What do you think I am? You get out and get it just like the rest of us. You ain't got no broke leg."

"I need my dress!" she demanded, her teeth clenched.

"We leaving!" he warned, his eyes shining with mischief. "You coming or not?"

She threatened him with a glare, her green eyes shooting daggers, and wrapping her arms around her chest, she emerged from the water, her camisole and panties molded against her skin.

She tied her pinafore with sharp deliberate tugs, her eyes daring him to speak, and with the last string in place, she took off in a run. Bounding close behind her, Crip followed, chuckling to himself.

Back at the house, they found Ms. Ambrose waiting in the yard.

"Where you been?" she demanded. "Off gallivanting when there's chores to be done! Wasting good daylight hours! I got a good mind to take a strap to the lot of you!"

Gracie snubbed softly, and Ms. Ambrose grabbed the child's arm and twisted it roughly behind her back. "Stop that sniffling or I give you something to cry about! I ask you where you been?"

Crip extended his hand to Gracie, his eyes never leaving Ms. Ambrose's face, his voice the quietness of death. "It's ok, baby girl," he encouraged. "Come over here and stand by me."

But Ms. Ambrose refused to let go of the Gracie's arm.

Everything about him demonstrated purpose, his jaw clamped shut, his eyes fixated, his fists clenched at his sides, and there was little doubt the actions he would take if Ms. Ambrose did not release the child. Unshaken, he voiced his intention, emphasizing each word, *"I said take your hand off her!"*

Nervously, Ms. Ambrose spat on the ground. "You and your smart mouth!" she said, releasing her hold on the child and shoving her forward. "You younguns get on about your chores! Get on, now!"

Crip put a protective arm around Gracie, gently urging all the children in the direction of the cornfield. "Come on, y'all," he said. "The quicker we get it started, the quicker we get it done."

Ms. Ambrose put her foot in his path. "Not you! You go find Bruce!"

Unable to suppress a gasp, Rebecca placed her hand on Crip's arm.

Ms. Ambrose turned on them. "What you waiting for? I said scram! And don't a one of you come back til it's all done!"

"It's ok," Crip nodded encouragingly. "Take the kids to the field. Ain't no need everbody getting in trouble."

All afternoon, Rebecca watched anxiously for Crip to join them. She found it hard to concentrate as she went about the chores, her mind on the cruelty he was sure to face.

"Where you think he is?" asked Teddy. "What's taking him so long?"

"You think he left us?" asked Michael.

"He ain't gone!" Gracie's voice pleaded for reassurance. "Is he, Becca?"

"I don't know no more'n you do, baby," she answered. "But, I guess we all know soon enough."

All afternoon, they took turns hoeing and carrying water for the long rows of corn, and when the field lay tended, they headed for the house. Tired and blistered, they wanted to rest, but the chores were not finished yet.

"Michael, you and Teddy go get that kindling Crip chop this morning and put it on the back porch. She pitch one more dilly that time you left it outside and it got rained on. Gracie, baby, you go with Butch to gather eggs, and do be careful with em."

"Yes ma'am," Gracie said, taking Butch's hand and leading him down the path to the henhouse.

"Bobby, take Joe with you to the sprang and fetch water, and make shore the bucket is full this time."

Without question, the seven-year-old twins grabbed a pail and headed down the hill, Bobby's head rising a good two inches above Joe's, his frame outweighing his brother by ten pounds.

Having lost their mother two days after they were born, their father had dropped the boys off at Sweet Haven before packing up and skipping the county. One certificate accompanied them, and Bobby Joe Peters was the only name printed on the document. Ms. Ambrose had said it was of no consequence, Joe being a frail and sickly infant who stood little chance to see his first birthday, but against all odds, Joe did survive, so she split the name between them. Joe was never a step from his brother's shadow, a nervous child, stuttering terribly, and when he became upset, he could not put his words together at all.

The rest of the afternoon, Rebecca's thoughts raced, her mind on Crip.

What would they do if he left them? It was a horrifying thought, and she tried to brush it from her mind. She didn't want to admit it, but she had come to rely on him as much as the children did.

He wouldn't leave, she told herself.

But, what if he did?

She went to the kitchen and started a fire in the cook stove, mixing a pan of cornpone and warming a pot of leftover beans and rice. A teakettle filled with water whistled, and Rebecca called them to supper, all the while, keeping her eyes glued to the doorway.

Alone in the kitchen, she poured hot water over a pan of dirty plates, and when she heard the click of a door-latch, she looked up, breathing a sigh of relief as Crip seemed to be unharmed.

He came to her, and grabbing a towel, he dried dishes and placed them on a shelf over the cabinet.

"You hungry?" she whispered. "I saved you a plate."

Barely acknowledging her, he shook his head.

"You ok?"

Big Bruce watched from the doorway, a warning look on his face.

"Crip?" she asked again.

His voice brisk, his manner insolent, Crip snapped, "Why don't you just mind your own business!"

"Well, it ain't like I care!" she retorted, hurt by the tone in his voice.

He touched her arm, his eyes pleading. "Just mind your business this time. Okay? Just this once."

Rebecca figured he was shamed by the punishment, and she resolved not to pressure him about it. If he wanted her to know, he would tell her.

Year of 1906

A year went by, twelve months without serious conflict, and peace dwelled within the orphanage. The children had found solace in Crip's presence, and Ms. Ambrose avoided confrontation with him as the children avoided her.

The youngsters looked to Crip with high regard, not only as their savior, but a friend. They had all flourished under his guidance and protection, and with a light in their eyes and a song in their hearts, they romped through fields of fescue, their shouts of laughter the sound of music for the soul.

He provided them with strong leadership and responsibility, and at the end of the day, he wooed them with vivid tales of adventure and courage. Having a creative imagination and a knack for flair, he entertained them with a nasty snarl and a stomp of his foot, acting out the roles of good guys and evil characters. Spellbound, the children held their breath in suspense as the story played out, fascinated by his ability to play both villain and hero.

As their mentor, Crip had formed a special bond with each of the children. Joe had left his brother's shadow, shocking them all with his interest in subjects too advanced for his age and lack of education. Crip found the lad surprisingly intelligent, and he did the best he could to supply the boy with knowledgeable answers to feed his hungry mind.

Having been responsible for his brother all their lives, Bobby had the mindset of an old man. A solemn and dependable child, he missed

Joe tagging along in his footsteps, and at first, had resented his brother's new-found confidence and certitude. But, through Crip's direction and incentive, Bobby had managed to acquire his own identity and was learning to appreciate the carefree days of childhood.

It warmed Rebecca's heart to see Crip's adoration of Gracie. He had come across a short log, one end bearing a strange resemblance of a head, and had spent hours whittling it into shape, carving a face and wrapping it in a scruffy blanket. He often played house with her, and Gracie delighted in his pretended fatherhood.

Michael, a tomboy, never cared about playing house. She ran with the fellows and was happiest when she was climbing trees or wrestling with them. Following Crip's instruction, she caught on quickly the art of simple twists and turns, nearly always triumphing over her rivals. The boys often tried to slip away without her, as it just was not fitting for a girl to be able to outdo them in everything.

With the curiosity of a cat, Teddy was the inquisitor of the group. He pumped his peers with intrusive questions, tactlessly interrogating them on matters of a sensitive nature or personal doings. He probed relentlessly to find answers to the many puzzles of life, exercising a belief that nothing happened without justifiable cause, and he let nothing deter him from getting to the heart of a matter. Once, he asked Crip his reasons for coming to Sweet Haven, and for days, he meditated over the answer, "To make people like you ask questions."

It was Butch that held Rebecca's concern. While the other children played, he sat from a distance, seemingly, content to watch. Sometimes, Rebecca thought she caught a glimpse of interest in his eyes, and she tried to encourage him to join the others in their antics, but he quietly refused. He'd shake his head and cover his mouth to suppress a giggle, satisfied within the realm of his own little world. At times, Rebecca spotted him and Crip sitting off by themselves, neither talking at all, yet bonding in friendship that went beyond words.

Impressed by his influence and control, Rebecca, too, looked to Crip with growing admiration. While he tended the outdoor chores, she tended the house and children, and with more time for herself, she started taking a new interest in her appearance.

She had started her womanly flow, and at first, had been too scared and mortified to tell anyone, but unsure if she would live, her fear of dying outweighed her shame, and she had approached Ms. Ambrose with her concerns.

Humiliated, she couldn't look the old woman in the eye. "I been bleeding," she said, her eyes downcast.

"You hurt?"

Rebecca gestured to her dilemma.

"It's about time," the old woman said, dismissing her without concern. "How old are you now . . . sixteen?"

"Near that. Another two months."

"You just got your sick time, that's all. You late getting started, but that don't matter none. Just count it a blessing . . . you don't get many in this life."

Rebecca waited for further instruction, and Ms. Ambrose waved her away. "Well, go on, now, don't just stand there! A woman keeps such as that to theirself. You'll figure it all out soon enough."

Rebecca left the room, and through the closed door, Ms. Ambrose yelled, "And, you stay clear of that boy! We got enough younguns running around here as it is!"

Rebecca soon came to understand that her ailment was not terminal, as it seemed to follow a pattern, usually right before the full moon cycled. She did the best she could to deal with it, and on these days, she avoided Crip, and he, suspecting her affliction, left her alone.

Early one morning on his round of chores, Crip was surprised by a young gelding wandering in the field. While the chickens clucked around his feet, a cluster of birds flew up from their nesting, and straining to see what had startled them, he spotted the colt grazing in the meadow. Trembling with excitement, he inched his way through the tall grass to get a better look, and when the horse was only feet away, he whistled softly to get the animal's attention.

Merely glancing toward the sound, the animal continued to graze in the open range.

Rushing back to the barn, Crip filled a pail with sweet oats, and cautiously, he eased his way back to the gelding. "Hey there, boy," he said, speaking in low, even tones. "What are you doing here?"

He set the bucket in front of the horse, and careful not to spook the creature, he ran his hand down the length of his back. With the bucket of tasty treats, he lured the four-legged critter back to the barn, and leaving him with his nose buried inside the pail, Crip ran to the kitchen.

"Come on!" he said, grabbing Rebecca by the hand. "Everbody! Hurry! I got something to show you!"

As they neared the barn, he warned, "Shh! Don't make no sudden noise."

At sight of the horse, Butch's eyes grew wide, and unable to contain his excitement, he blurted, "It's Christmas!"

It was the first time he had spoken without encouragement, and Rebecca's eyes brimmed with tears. Without thinking, Crip reached for her hand and softly squeezed her fingers.

Inside the stall, the horse nibbled at his trough, indifferent to his audience.

"Can we keep her?" asked Michael.

"He ain't a girl," Crip told her. "And, I don't know about keeping him. Depends."

"Depends on what?" asked Teddy.

"Well, we don't know who he belongs to," Crip explained. "But, I guess if nobody claims him, he's ours to keep."

Excitedly, Gracie squealed, "Hide him!"

"Yeah!" they all clamored.

"Shh!" Rebecca warned. "Don't scare him, now. But, it wouldn't be right to hide him. He come here by hisself and I guess he'll leave by hisself if he's got a mind to go. We'll just leave him be and let him do the deciding. We don't want him here if he don't wanna stay. I wouldn't wish that on nobody, and I know you wouldn't neither. Now, let's get back in the house afore we all get in trouble."

Eager to get back to the wonder in the barn, they gulped down their breakfast and in record time, finished their chores and headed for the shed.

Corralling around the stall, they all talked at once. "Where he come from, Crip?" asked Bobby.

"Don't know. Maybe Butch is right. Maybe it is Christmas and he's a reindeer and just got lost."

"He ain't no reindeer!" Teddy scoffed. Taking a closer look, he wondered aloud, "Is he?"

"He's purty, ain't he?" piped Gracie.

"Yeah, he be purty, alright. Somebody took good care of him."

"How old you th-think he is?" asked Joe.

"Don't know that answer."

"Do you think he like us?" asked Bobby.

"Don't know that, neither, but he ain't scared of us," Crip answered. "Looky here, he'll eat right out of my hand."

"If he's gonna stay here, he be needing a name," Rebecca said.

"Yeah, you right. Everbody pick a name and we take a vote on it," Crip instructed.

"S-S-Star?" Joe stuttered.

Crip quickly agreed. "He does have a star on his forehead."

"Moon?" asked Teddy, scowling when they laughed.

"What about Clover?" asked Michael.

"That sounds good, too," Crip told her. "I found him in the clover patch."

"Midnight," Butch whispered.

"Midnight! Now, I like that! What you all think?" Crip asked.

"Purty Boy!" exclaimed Gracie.

"They all good names," Rebecca said. "But, he can't have all of em. We got to pick one."

"I like Midnight," Crip said, tousling Butch's hair.

Rebecca was ready to agree when she saw the look on Joe's face.

"He's got to have two names just like everbody does. How about we name him Midnight Star?" Rebecca suggested, draping her arm around Joe's shoulders.

"Yeah, that's good!" they all agreed. "Midnight Star!"

The colt never left and no one ever claimed him, and the children figured he was just like them, an orphan, and seemed only natural that he ended up at Sweet Haven.

Rebecca paused from her chores, her attention drawn to the laughter floating through the open window.

In the front yard, four flat rocks mapped out a diamond-shaped course, and Crip ran the distance, touching each one with his foot before moving to the next. The children watched, their shouts of cheer urging him to go faster.

Puzzled, Rebecca asked, "What on earth is going on out here?"

"We getting up a ball team!" Teddy explained. "Crip's showing us the rules."

Out of breath, Crip bounded to the porch. "Wanna play?" he puffed. "Be boys against girls."

"That don't seem fair. Girls is outnumbered."

"Well, since me and you the oldest, we'll choose sides, and just to be fair, I take Gracie from the get-go. That orta even things out some."

"Is this a real game or did you make it up?" she asked doubtfully.

"Yeah, it's real. It's plenty fun, too."

"How's it go?"

"Well, it goes like this . . . all you do is take this here stick, and when somebody throws the ball at you, you try to hit it. And, if you hit it, then you run like hell and try to touch that rock over there, and if you don't hit it, you out. And when your team gets out three times, the other side takes a turn. That's all there is to it."

"I don't know. It just don't seem fair to me, you with the upper hand and all . . . already knowing how to play."

"Sounds to me like somebody's scared of getting beat," he taunted.

"Boy, them's fighting words!" she challenged. "Start the picking."

Rebecca's team came up first, and Michael stood at bat, a determined look on her face. Crip threw the ball, and she swung with all her strength, but it whizzed by her.

"Strike one!" he yelled.

He drew back and let go of the ball, but this time, Michael was ready for him. She swung the stick, hitting the ball so hard it ricocheted off the banister and rolled across the yard.

Cheering loudly, all the children scrambled for the ball.

"Everbody on Rebecca's team get back over here!" Crip instructed the trespassers. "You got to remember which side you on!"

Sheepishly, they reclaimed their places, and Rebecca stepped up to bat.

Crip took his time, ducking his head to hide a mischievous smirk. He stretched his arms, stomped the plate, and spit a couple of times before drawing back and letting go, aiming the ball well over her head.

"How you spect me to hit it if you can't throw a straight line?"

"You gotta keep your eye on the ball!" he yelled, and winding his arm, he threw the second ball low to the ground.

"Is that the best you can do?" she asked.

"Make up your mind!" he taunted, throwing another foul and declaring her out. "It's too high, it's too low . . . what else do you want me to do?"

"Learn how to throw a ball would be a good start."

"Let's see if you can do any better," he told her, grinning like a Cheshire cat. "It's time to change sides."

Rebecca handed him the bat, uttering under her breath, "I never took you to be a cheater. It's just a game."

"Aw, don't be such a sore loser," he hissed. "You just stand back. Watch me, and let a man show you how it's done."

The ball was an easy mark for him, and with little effort, he sent it sailing into the trees. He placed his hand above his eyes to watch it disappear, and with a wide grin, he turned to Rebecca, tipped his hat and took a bow.

She studied him, a smile on her lips. He was good with the children . . . good for them. He was good for her.

Before the afternoon ended, they all knew the rules of the game, at least, the rules according to Crip, although Rebecca swore he made them up as the game played out. But, it was a fun game, and at the end of every day, they could hardly wait until the chores were finished to play again.

Autumn came early, and before cold weather set in, another meeting was summoned at the creek. While the children ran about, Rebecca and Crip settled on a pile of leaves beneath a tree.

He shifted his weight to get comfortable, and his pants inched up his leg, baring a deep red scar. She had seen that scar before when they swam in the creek, but had not mentioned it for fear of embarrassing him. Now, she felt she knew him well enough to pose the question how it all came about.

"Crip, what happened to your leg? And I don't want to hear nothing about you being born like that. I seen the scars."

"It's a long story and I ain't got that much time," he answered, pulling at his pants to hide the ugly mark.

"I'd like to know why it is you can yak up a storm til it comes to something about you," she fussed. "Then, all a sudden like, you ain't got nothing to say."

"I got plenty to say. You shore you wanting to hear?"

"I ask you, didn't I?"

"Well, listen up then, cause I ain't saying it but once, and after that, we ain't talking about it no more. It was like this . . . times was bad and luck was running out . . . hell, ain't no two ways about it, I was starving when this old man seen me and took me home with him. Soon as I walked in, he sets me down at this here table just loaded with biscuits and beans and stuff. I didn't know what to think, but his missus, Miz Betty, she a purty good cook and I was purty hungry, so I didn't waste no time tearing into the vittles. After I eat my fill, I was real oblige like, and so I offer back by asking him if he needing any help. He laugh like a hyena and say what did I think he brung me here for. Turns out, he was mean as hell, straight from the Klux, and the only reason he brung me home with him in the first place was to work the farm. I don't know why he call it a farm, cause it wouldn't grow weeds. And, nothing I did never please him, and nothing never growed neither. The land was barren and cold and bitter . . . just like him.

"I guess I might have been about eleven at the time, and a kid can just do so much, and like I say, he was mean, but when he got to drinking, well, he was a brother to the devil hisself. Miz Betty, she try to take care of me some . . . she the one who learnt me to read and stuff . . . and like I say, she try, but I guess when he was beating on me, he was leaving her alone, so she didn't step up much. It happened about a year after he took me in. He been hitting the bottle purty hard for a week, and I guess I done something he didn't like . . . which didn't take much to do . . . and he beat me up real bad. I'd had enough of that, and so I took it on myself to try and get away. I waited til night come when I knowed he would be asleep, and I slip out the winder, trying to keep quiet and all. It was dark as hell out there, and I fell over a bucket. It made an awful racket, and the old man woke up. I seen him coming, a flashlight in one hand and a big stick in the other, and I tried to hide best I could, but it was too late. He done seen me, and . . ." he stopped, a faraway look in his eyes as the memory of that night flooded back, "and nothing Miz Betty could say would make him let up on me. He beat me til I couldn't stand up. And, that's the whole of it."

"That's just awful! When did you leave there?"

"When I come here."

"But, how did you get away?"

He shook his head. "Some things are better not said. Don't matter, no how. I'm here now, not that this place is too much better, but I ain't no kid no more. Ain't nobody never going to beat me again! Nobody! And, they ain't going to be hurting nobody else neither. Not while I got breath."

Hesitantly, she asked, "Big Bruce?"

"That big old pussy cat? Why, he ain't never hurt nobody. He just has to act like he does cause old Ambrose would get rid of him if she knowed. That's why nobody talks about it, and the old bitch thinks everthing went her way."

Rebecca was astonished. All these years she had lived in fear of Bruce, and as it turned out, there had been nothing to fear but fear itself. She could not believe the children had never told her the truth.

"Was you ever in a real home?" she asked.

"Yeah. I use to live with Granny," he said, a grin spreading across his face with fond memories. "She was something else, my old Granny! She didn't care what other folks did . . . she had her own way of doing things, and we did things Granny's way. And, she always say that if you hurt somebody cause they was hurting you or somebody else, then it ain't wrong. Ain't nobody got a right to lay a hand on you, and if they do, then it's a tooth for a tooth. That's what Granny always say."

"Where's Granny at now?"

"She got T.B. and died. At first, I got sent from one house to another'n, and I'd stay there with em til they got tired of me being in the way, and then, they'd send me someplace else, and it didn't take long til there wouldn't no place else to go. Having used up all my welcomes, I knocked around here and there for a while, stole stuff out of people's gardens in the summer, slept anywhere I could. That's how the old son-of-a-bitch find me . . . sleeping under a tree, half out of my mind, my guts sticking to my back, and it didn't take too much coaxing to get me to go with him."

"How long in all did you stay there with that mean old man and Miz Betty?"

"Too long," he said. "I done said enough, and I ain't talking about that no more. Let's get these younguns back to the house afore that damn old bitch starts wailing again."

"My goodness, Crip! If I didn't know better, I'd swear you was a preacher's son! If you don't stop all that cussing, I ain't going to hang around you no more! Why, I'm scared to get close to you for fear the devil might throw down a ball of fire, and I don't wanna get hit . . . not when you be the one he's after!"

"I try and weigh it down a little, but dammit, it's a poor time when a man can't say what he feels! And anyways, Granny always say it ain't cussing if you don't put God's name in it, and you don't hear me saying that!"

"Well, just in case Granny's wrong, you go set over there next to that bucket of water, cause I ain't taking no chances!"

Laughing, he stood up and pulled her to her feet. "Come on, skinny angel! Get your younguns and let's go."

Like a thundering herd, they ran back to the house, whooping as they cut through the forest.

Year of 1907

Spring of nineteen hundred and seven arrived with renewed hope and attitude, and a late-blooming seventeen-year-old Rebecca had developed into a young woman-child almost overnight. She took notice the budding breasts straining through her shirts, hips rounding in a definitive curve, a fleshy, firm derriere, and delightfully pleased by her new appearance, she often practiced in front of the broken mirror the way that she should walk, stand, purse her lips and smile.

She spent hours preparing meals that gained Crip's praise, secretly pretending he was her husband and the children, theirs. She strove to please him, frying potatoes with the peelings, adding shallots to a pan of cornpone, and baking apple pie, as apple was his favorite. In every sense of the word, she played the role of housewife, and it was only at night when she climbed into her bed that the character left her feeling empty and incomplete.

Rebecca was not the only one mindful of her new attractive look. Lately, Crip found her consuming his thoughts throughout the day, and at night, his dreams swept him to the edge of execution, leaving him troubled, frustrated and unfulfilled.

The two had become inseparable, and although they had not spoken aloud of their feelings, the very air around them whispered of intimacy. He often read to her, the stories relaying a world far away from Sweet Haven, portraying a perfect picture of a wonderful life, of undying love, and of happiness ever after.

Early June, Crip sat comfortably on the porch reading aloud from a book of fairytales, Rebecca at his side and the children clustered at his feet.

"And they all live happy ever after," he finished, closing the book with a snap.

"Read another'n," they begged.

"That's enough reading for one day. You all run on and see if you can't catch a few lightning bugs afore you have to turn in."

Rebecca was unusually quiet, and he watched her for a moment before invading her thoughts. "You awful still. What are you thinking about?"

"You think that's the way it really is?" she asked, dreamy-eyed.

"What?"

"Love and happy ever after?"

"Well, love is, anyways. I ain't too shore about the happy part."

"How do you know what love feels like?"

He shrugged.

"Have you ever felt like that afore?" she asked, stiffening.

"Yeah, I have," he answered softly. "You ain't?"

Quickly, she looked away and shook her head.

He pushed her hair behind her ear to peer at her. "Are you shore about that?"

"Are you?" she asked, jealously nipping at her heart.

"Didn't I say it? Wouldn't be a thing to lie about."

"When?" she demanded to know. "And, with who?"

Grinning, he averted his eyes. "If you don't know, I ain't going to be the one to tell you. I didn't take you for no dumb girl."

She tossed her head, pretending indifference. "No dumber'n you, and just like always, you yak about things you don't know nothing about."

"If you going to open that mouth of yours and spit seeds, then you better talk what you know," he said smugly. "There's a lot of stuff I know that you ain't even thought about."

"What kind of stuff?"

"Stuff like what goes on between a man and a woman . . . that kind of stuff."

Her eyes sparkled with interest. "Tell me what you know!"

"Well now," he drawled, "I don't know that I should. What if you ain't ready for it?"

"I'm ready for it!" she declared. "Now, tell me! And, don't leave nothing out!"

"Well, for starters," he began, eager to educate her in acts of the heart, "there's two things, love and desire. They ain't the same thing, but most folks can't tell the difference, not til it's too late. Now, either one is good, but it's better if you can get both of em. This thing . . . desire . . . it's a sneaky old thing! It comes upon you real sudden like, and you get to feeling like you can't breathe, like you got a big old rock setting on your chest and your heart's about to jump out. You wanna say something, but your mouth won't move. Then, all a sudden like, your muscles start acting crazy, jerking and stuff, and you ain't even trying to make em! And, your eyes start looking funny, too, like you can't see what's in front of you . . . kinda like . . ." He paused in mid-sentence, and frowning, he looked closely into her eyes. "Kinda like yourn do now!"

Quickly, she turned away. "If it be like all that, you can keep that desire for yourself. I shore won't be looking for it! Sounds like you be dying!"

"Well, you ain't got no choice about it. You ain't got to look for it . . . you ain't even got to think about it. When you least expect it, it'll find you. Might be the way somebody looks at you or something they say. It don't take much, and boom!" he said, slapping his hands together. "There it is . . . desire!"

Swallowing hard, she dropped her eyes, afraid that he might be right. "How you know all this?"

"I got my ways. Now, love," he continued, settling back on the porch, "love is something else, a whole different thing. Love don't happen all at once, but it can be just as sneaky. You can be around somebody everday and not know, and one day you look at em, and it's like you ain't never even seen em afore. When it's love you feeling, your heart feels like it's going to bust open, but it's a good feeling. It makes you wanna do good things . . . like help em carry stuff, and take care of em, and give em everthing they want. And, if they ain't with you ever minute, it feels like something is missing, like you just a little piece of something and you can't be whole without em."

He watched her out of the corner of his eye. "You shore you ain't never feel nothing like that?"

Without answering, she slid closer and eased her hand in his. They sat quietly, scarcely breathing, and when the last traces of sun disappeared over the horizon, he called the children to bed. Reluctantly, she let go of his hand and followed them inside.

The first day of summer was hot, and the children begged for a meeting at the creek. Eager to test the water, Teddy kicked off his shoes and unsnapped the straps of his overalls. As he wrestled to pull his shirt over his head, Rebecca stopped him.

"You ain't getting in that creek so don't even think about it," she instructed. "It'll be another month before that water is ready for swimming."

"But it's hot as shit out here!" he argued.

"Boy, you better watch that mouth!" Crip told him, quickly turning away to hide a snicker.

"Why can't we go swimming?" Teddy whined.

"Cause I said so, that's why," Rebecca answered with authority. "Just cause the sun is hot don't mean creek water is. You step one foot in that water this early in the year and you apt to get sick."

Scowling, they all ran off, but were soon playing happily in and out among the brush. Rebecca found a comfortable spot beneath the tree, and frowning, she turned to Crip. "You know, they get that from you."

"What's that?"

"Talking like they do, using words that they ain't got no business saying."

"They just being younguns, that's all," he defended them.

"That's what I mean. They are younguns, and them ain't words younguns need to be saying. You neither, far as that goes."

"Did you come here to preach? I thought this was spose to be the one place where we could come and just be ourself."

"It is," she said, "but when they go talking like that, they ain't being theirself . . . they trying to be like you. It just don't sound right coming from a youngun."

"No? Well, you could've fooled me cause I thought it sounded purty funny."

"Yeah, you would. But, I would have boxed his jaws for talking like that, only I can't do it with you standing right in front of him laughing about it."

"Aw, Teddy's ok. He ain't no dumb kid, and if saying shit is the worst thing he ever does, then he'll be alright."

"I guess. Come here, Crip. Set next me and read me something good."

"Shore thing," he said, pulling a worn, faded book of poetry from his back pocket. "What you wanna hear?"

"Anything."

He dropped down beside her, and she leaned her head on his shoulder while he sorted through the yellowed pages. "Here's a good one," he said, clearing his throat.

"Angel of my Heart

All alone, her striking beauty
Stood out from all the rest
She wore a halo on her head
Her clothes, an angel's dress.

And, the minute that I saw her
None other could compare
To that purty little maiden
That held me prison there.

As precious as a diamond
As rare as a pearl
Worth more than gold and silver
Was this fair-skinned maiden girl.

And, I want so much to hold her
To feel her in my arms
I want so much to kiss her
I truly meant no harm.

She was like a dainty flower
Her petals soft and sweet
And I didn't know I hold her so
Til she lay there at my feet.

Oh, I would die ten times o'er
A thousand if it would
Bring back the fair-skinned maiden
But, my death would do no good.

So, behind these walls I do my time
Cold, alone and dark
And, here I be til again I see
The angel of my heart."

Rebecca listened closely to the disturbing tale of unrequited love. She wasn't sure why, but the poem made her feel sad, and mulling it over, she asked, "Is that poem about love or desire?"

Stuffing the book in his back pocket, he asserted, "Well, it ain't love. Love hurts sometimes, but not on purpose."

"Love hurts? How?"

"Well, for one thing, like you wanting to box Teddy's jaws a while ago. If you didn't love him, you wouldn't give a never mind to what he says, but I'll bet if you got Teddy's take on it, he'd say it hurt like hell."

She pondered his words of wisdom and was about to pose another question, when suddenly, he jumped to his feet, an impish glint in his eye.

"Come on!" he dared, grabbing her by the arm. "Let's see how cold that water is!"

"No!" she exclaimed, and breaking free from his grip, she jumped behind the tree, dodging his reach.

He chased her in circles, and when she darted to the forest, Crip followed close on her heels. Catching up, he wrapped his arms around her and pulled her to the creek bank.

"Don't, Crip!" she shrieked, digging her heels in the soil. "Please don't do it!"

In her scramble to get away, she fell to the ground, and in an instant, he was on top of her, his weight pinning her to the ground.

She struggled to become free, each twisting movement magnifying her consciousness of him, and involuntarily, her body responded, stirring her to unrest. She stopped struggling, and without a thought, turned her face to his.

It was barely a touch, yet the world seemed to stop when his lips grazed hers. Her mind spinning, she closed her eyes, expectantly waiting. The silence of time stretched into forever, and her eyes fluttered open to find him watching her, his face pained, his eyes questioning. Gently, he brushed her hair away from her face, moistened his lips and leaned in.

Her breath caught in anticipative suspense, and she lifted her lips to meet his, but instead of a kiss, he pressed his mouth against her ear.

"Gotcha . . ." he whispered, and jumping up, he ran off to join the others.

Breathlessly embarrassed, she turned to look at him. He was waiting for her, and she put her hand to her mouth, smiling shyly, her heart aquiver. Leisurely, she brushed the grass from her skirt, and sauntering to him, she broke into a run and didn't stop until she reached the house.

That night was filled with restless dreams, and every time she turned over in her bed, she could hear him moving about in the room next to hers.

Young love flourished, and it was soon common knowledge that Crip would marry her one day. That decision had been determined on September afternoon at the creek while sitting under their tree.

Crip pulled the book of poetry from his pocket, and she smiled, always ready to hear him recite from his collection of mystically woven tales. She loved the sound of his voice, the words trickling over his tongue as a gurgling brook, and lost in the quote of simple rhymes, she closed her eyes, her imagination escorting her to faraway places where ladies and gentlemen, dressed in Sunday's best, sipped tea while idling away the afternoon.

He stopped reading to look at her, her face glowing in dreamy wonderment, and overwhelmed with a sudden urge to kiss her, he dropped the book to the ground. He pulled her to him, forcing his tongue inside her mouth, his hand, inadvertently, resting against her breast.

Flushed, she jumped up, her cheeks rosy with embarrassment. "What you think you doing? You can't touch me like that! Ain't but one man got that right, and that's the man I marry!"

Lazily, he stood up and shoved the book in his back pocket. "And who else do you think you going to marry asides me?" he drawled, avoiding her eyes.

She was taken aback by his words. "Are you asking to marry me?"

He kept his back to her, seeming to take more interest in the sparrow building a nest in a nearby tree than her response. "Well now," he shrugged, "that all depends. Are you saying yeah?"

She didn't respond right away, and he turned to face her. "It's the only offer you get from me. Take it or leave it. I don't ask for nothing twice."

He made light of it, but somehow, she knew he spoke in earnest. "I take it," she told him, matter-of-factly.

It was an uncomfortable moment, each waiting for the other, unsure what should happen next. Uneasily, she spoke first, "Ain't you spose to give me something to seal it?"

Her request took him by surprise. He had nothing to offer her, nothing except his treasured book of poems, and abashed, he pulled it from his pocket and handed it to her.

"Here," he said sheepishly. "It's all I got, and anyways, it says everthing I want to say but don't know how."

Feeling both amused and compassionate by his show of bashfulness, she smiled encouragingly. "I think you do all right," she said softly. "You know, with saying what you want and all."

She stood there beneath the tree, a sweet smile on her face and her arms wrapped around the book, and he stood not two feet away, wishing he could tell her the words in his heart . . . wanting to kiss her the way he wanted to *be* kissed . . . to take her in his arms and hold her until day turned to night and night again to morn, but knowing the consequences such actions would surely bring about, he took a deep breath and eased back into his usual banter. "Well, now, I give you something. Don't you think turn-about's fair play?"

"I don't know what you spect to get from me. I ain't got nothing to give."

"You got lips, don't you?"

"But, you done had a kiss . . ."

"You call *that* a kiss? That wouldn't nothing but a little old chicken peck. A real kiss is when two people both take part. Anything less and you might as well be kissing a pole. If that's what you call a kiss, you can keep it til you can do better."

Pouting, her mouth fell open, and he rushed to make amends. "Ain't no need getting all vexed. I'm just funning with you. I didn't want no kiss, no how."

"Yeah, you did," she declared blatantly.

He threw his head back and laughed. "Let's go see what them younguns are up to."

They strolled up the creek bank, and suddenly, she turned to him. "What's your real name, Crip? I think I got a right to know the name of the man I'm going to marry, and I know Crip ain't it."

He had stopped to skip a pebble across the water, and at her question, he scowled. "Ash Lee . . . Ash Lee Chaney."

"Rebecca Chaney," she mumbled. "Rebecca and Ash Lee Chaney. That's got a right good sound to it."

"Ain't nothing wrong with Crip, and as for the other, keep it to yourself. Nobody calls me that no more."

"How you come to be called Crip? And, afore you go lying again," she warned, "I already know it ain't like you say, neither."

"You shore do ask an awful lot of questions. All a sudden like, I ain't too shore I wanna marry a nosy girl."

"Oh, I think you purty shore. But, you can keep it to yourself, cause I don't give a hoot, no how!"

"Oh, you give a hoot, alright. You ain't never been one for letting things be. But, it's like this . . . when I was a little boy, about two or so, I guess . . . there was a creek that run longside the house, and ever time I went missing, that's where Granny would find me. Being a baby and all, I couldn't talk too good, and I call it the *crip*, and so I got dub with it. Take it or leave it."

She thought he might be lying again, but she nodded, satisfied with his answer. "I take it."

They called the children together, and while the young ones raced back to the house ahead of them, Crip and Rebecca lagged behind. He slipped his arm around her waist, and it was not until they reached the edge of the forest that he let her go.

After that, he couldn't stay away from her. Sometimes, he would surprise her, sneaking up behind her just to catch the scent of musk from her skin and the sweet mixture of magnolia blossoms and lemon in her hair, and he yearned to touch her.

Feeling his presence, she'd turn around abruptly, purposefully brushing against him, the thoughts running through her mind flushing her face with color. She did nothing to discourage him, hopefully waiting for him to make another bold move.

But, he didn't . . . and she dared not.

"C-C-Come!" Joe shouted, bounding through the woods.

Alarmed, Rebecca and Crip sprang from their seat beneath the tree. "What is it?"

"M-Michael's b-bleeding!"

"Where is she?"

"D-Down there by the c-creek!"

Following on Joe's heels, they rushed through the forest where they found Michael weeping uncontrollably.

"What's wrong, baby?" Rebecca asked, her voice edged with concern. "You bleeding? Where you hurt?"

"She won't say nothing!" Bobby explained. "We asked her what's wrong, and she won't talk. She just cries . . . that's all she does!"

Gracie too, began to weep softly, and Teddy gestured with his hands, palms up. "What's wrong with *her* now?"

"She's just scared, Teddy," Rebecca told him. "Move out of the way and let me see what I can do."

"Michael ain't going to die, is she?" he blurted.

Teddy shrugged at Rebecca's glare, and she tried again to unravel the situation, speaking softly so as not to upset the girl further. "Talk to me, Michael. Where you hurt?"

But, Michael only sobbed harder.

Feeling that privacy might lend a hand in getting to the bottom of the issue, Rebecca motioned the children away. Crip took Gracie by the hand, and Rebecca could hear her wailing as they ambled down the path. "Don't let her die! Please don't let her die!"

When they were out of earshot, Rebecca tried again. "Where you hurt, honey? Ain't nothing I can do about it if you don't tell me."

"Am I going to die?" Michael whimpered.

"No!" Rebecca declared, praying this would not be another lie she told. "Come on, now, baby, show me where you hurt."

"I don't know! I wouldn't doing nothing . . . just playing over yonder . . . and when I looked down, I seen all this blood, and I don't know where it come from! I ain't got no cuts nor nothing . . . no scratches! I don't wanna die, Rebecca! What's wrong with me?"

"Let's get you back to the house where we can take a better look."

Having found no visible signs of injury, Rebecca supposed it might be the same suffering that had befallen her, but it seemed so unfair. Michael was barely ten.

Inside the house, Rebecca breathed a sigh of relief when she found her suspicions to be true. It was a slight imposition, but she would not die from it.

"It ain't nothing to be scared of, honey," she consoled her. "I was scared, too, when it happened to me. It just means you growing up, that's all. Let's get you washed up."

When the pair ventured outside, Crip rushed to Rebecca's side. "Is she alright?"

Rebecca shook her head in warning, and understanding the implications, he nodded knowingly.

"You still bleeding?" Teddy asked, all the while giving Michael the once-over.

"It's catching!" she threatened. "You best just stay away from me or you'll all get it!"

"Come with me, honey," Rebecca said, putting her arm around the girl's shoulders. "Let's go set on the porch a spell."

She brushed Michael's hair while she explained. "You be alright in a few days. Keep your eye out for when the moon gets full, and you got to be careful, now, how you set and all. Keep your dress down, and no more climbing trees. I guess you a woman, now, and you got to start acting like one."

"Do boys . . . do they . . ."

"No, baby. It's just the plight of a woman. A girl is like an old sore-tail cat, I guess, and boys are dogs. They might get a flea ever now and again, but that be about it."

And, having said that, Rebecca felt she had educated the girl with all the information necessary in becoming a woman.

Year of 1908

The middle of January brought a cold blast from the north, and a winter storm settled over Lando Ferry. With temperatures refusing to budge above freezing, icicles hung from the eaves, and the few logs left in the woodpile rapidly disappeared underneath a blanket of white precipitation.

Wind howled through the cracks in the walls, and in an effort to keep warm, the children spent long days inside crouched around a pot-bellied stove, and at night, they climbed into one bed, spooned against each other, their blankets compiled over their heads to shut out the eerie glow of embers and shadowy dancers on the wall.

The cellar lay bare, the cupboard empty, and for weeks, they had eaten nothing but cornpone and jam. Chilled to the bone, they barely noticed the rumble in their stomachs, too numb to feel anything, too cold to care.

Big Bruce rose early to make the long walk to town for supplies. The neighbors had been generous in the past, and the children watched out the window, anxiously awaiting his return.

Crip and Rebecca went to the barn, her thin jacket pulled tightly around her. Midnight Star had not been fed in days and they were fearful he might not make it another. She stroked his face, willing the love she felt for the animal to fill his empty stomach.

At the sound of clopping hooves, they rushed to the house to help unload an abundant supply of provisions strapped to the buckboard. A nice looking young man with a trim beard and gentle eyes stepped from the wagon, and shyly, Rebecca glanced in his direction. He appeared in his late twenties, rather tall and muscled, confident, yet simple in style.

With a favorable nod, he looked her over, a slight smile on his lips. It wasn't often that Rebecca saw a person of interest, and she smiled back, appreciative of his obvious approval.

When the wagon stood empty, he turned to her. "Name's Jesse Blevins," he nodded, offering his hand.

She felt his grip, strong and protective, and she curtsied, dropping her eyes. "Rebecca Mason," she murmured.

"I live right through them trees about a mile up the creek," he told her.

She nodded, not sure why he felt the need to tell her that.

"Sometime, if you up for it, maybe you'd like to come and set on the porch a spell? I could use the company, and it'd get you out some."

Blushing profusely, she looked away and quickly shook her head. "I reckon not."

"Maybe you'll change your mind. Maybe come spring when all this nasty weather is behind us, you'll see fit to visit."

She wasn't aware that he still held her hand until he let it go, his eyes scrolling behind her to the barn. Midnight Star stepped into the open, and he seemed to take a keen interest in the animal. "That be a fine looking horse you got there. Where'd you get him?"

"He's ours," she stated, unable to hide the nervous tremor in her voice.

"Is he, now?" he asked, starting for the barn.

She placed her hand on his arm to stop him, and curiously, he frowned. "How long have you had him?"

"He's ours, Mr. Blevins," she reaffirmed, and repeating herself, "He's ours!"

Jesse looked from her to the children waiting on the porch, cold and ragged, their eyes joyless, and in a voice overcome with compassion, he nodded, "Yeah, I guess he is, at that."

He reached into the buckboard, and sorting through his sacks, he offered Rebecca a bag of sweet oats. "Take this," he said. "Animals has got a way of straying off when they get to looking for something to eat, and right now, he looks like he might be ready for wandering."

"Thank you," she whispered, her eyes acknowledging his kindness. "It's awful good of you."

She reached for the bag, and he let her tug at it before letting go, his eyes teasing.

She blushed again, and he smiled. "Good day, Miss Rebecca."

She stood a moment to watch him ride away, grateful that he had not pressured her more about the animal.

"What'd he say to you?" Crip asked, coming up behind her.

She jumped at the sound of his voice. "Nothing really, but I think the horse is his."

"You don't say? Well, he might as well let that rest. Long as we've had him, it's too late to go laying claims now. He ain't getting him."

She sighed softly, both surprised and amused. "It ain't him he's wanting."

Spring finally arrived, a welcome change, and as the sun rose to warm the earth, the children rushed outdoors, eager to come out of hibernation and away from Ms. Ambrose.

Hitching a plow to Midnight Star, Crip walked along behind him, laying off rows for the garden. With rakes, shovels and hoes, the children worked diligently to prepare the soil for new seedlings, and after weeks of long, tiresome days, the garden lay tended. To celebrate, they summoned a meeting.

Rebecca had missed the gatherings at the creek. Through the long winter months of being cooped inside, Crip had become detached, often moody and abrupt. She had tried to talk to him, but the eye of Ms. Ambrose was constantly watching, and he had steered clear of the woman, unwilling to be the cause of her wrath.

Running up and down the creek bank, the children shouted in glee, and Rebecca and Crip laughed at their energy and resilience. They settled beneath the tree, and instantly, he was back to his old self, talking about the future and their lives together.

"One of these days soon," he told her, "I'm going to take you away from all this. We'll go anywhere you want . . . see things you won't never see around here. We'll get us a little land, build a house and . . ."

"With a white picket fence and a big fireplace?"

"If you want," he nodded. "We'll work longside each other fixing it up to suit us, you and me. We'll have a garden . . ."

"We'll grow big red maters, and corn, and green beans! And, ever year, we'll put enough food in jars to help see us through the winter!"

"That for shore," he agreed. "And, when we get everthing set just right, we'll have us a few younguns to run around the house and . . ."

"A whole passel of em! Six! I want three boys and three girls. And, I want em to have everthing they want, and I ain't never going to spank em or tell em there ain't nothing they can't do."

"Then, it ain't a houseful of younguns you'll have, but a houseful of spoilt scalawags," he warned. "Younguns tend to have a devilish streak, and they need a whooping once in a while to get it out of em."

"Not my younguns."

"I don't know, Angel. Kids will do whatever you let em, and sometimes they need a good smack on the backside just to keep their heads on straight."

"Oh, and that's another thing," she declared. "There ain't going to be no crooked heads in my house, neither, and if you so much as lift a finger to one of my babies, it's me you be dealing with!"

"You?" he scoffed. "Why, you ain't no more'n a little old honeybee."

Her eyes narrowed. "And you ain't never been stung, have you?"

He laughed out loud. "Red on the head . . . fire below?"

"What's that spose to mean?"

"Whatever you can make out of it. But, how's this sound to you . . . pet the girls all you want, but leave the boys to me. I ain't going to stand still for you mollycoddling our boys."

"Don't stand still, then," she said, brushing him off with a shrug of the shoulder. "Jump up and down, kick the walls and throw a real hissy-fit, and see what it gets you. My babies ain't getting no spankings, and that's that!"

"You know what you starting to sound like?" he grinned. "You starting to sound like an old married woman, all bossy and everthing. But, you can rest your mind about me smacking on our kids. They be my babies, too, and I ain't going to be hurting em none."

"I know you wouldn't," she smiled. "I want em to be just like you . . . the boys, anyhow, not so much the girls."

"I don't care what they be like as long as they got all their fingers and toes."

She dropped her head. "I love you, Crip," she whispered.

"I know you do. These past months has been hell, me trying to keep a distance atween us and you always right there. I missed being with you like this."

"Me too," she sighed. "Crip?"

"Yeah?"

"You and me . . . we always going to be together, ain't we?"

"You bet. For the rest of our lives."

"And, you wouldn't never leave me, would you?"

"No, Angel," he vowed with sincerity. "I wouldn't never do nothing to hurt you. Why you ask me this?"

"No reason, really. It's just . . . there ain't never been nothing good in my life til you come, and when I'm with you, I forget all about everthing bad that's ever happened. I got this feeling inside . . . a happy feeling . . . like everthing I ever want is mine, and sometimes, it scares me to feel this good. I get to thinking that something's bound to happen to mess it up . . . that it's just too good to last, and . . ."

"Rest easy, Sweet Angel, I ain't going nowhere . . . not without you. Looky here, I got something for you," he said, pulling a faded red rag from his pocket.

"What is it?" she asked.

He unfolded the cloth, and inside she found a whittled piece of wood, the wings rough and unshapely, but Rebecca thought it was the most beautiful angel she had ever seen.

"When did you do this?"

"I had to find something to keep me busy while I was shut up in the house all winter. I know it ain't too good," he apologized.

"No, you did good. It's real purty, Crip. Thank you." Sadly, she dropped her eyes. "I wish I had something to give you."

He studied her, his eyes mellow with emotion. "You do," he said softly.

She was almost afraid to breathe. "What do you want?"

"What do you think?" he asked, tilting her face to his, so close she could feel the warmth of him, the tremble inside him, the very beat of his heart.

Her lips parted to taste him, and from out of nowhere, Teddy appeared. "What y'all doing?" he asked suspiciously.

"What's it look like?" Crip scowled, throwing a handful of leaves at him.

Innocently, Teddy shrugged. "I dunno. Looky here, Crip, see what I found. I got this big old worm from over there. There's plenty more of em, too. Wanna go get some? Be good for fishing."

"Sometimes I could ring that boy's neck," Crip muttered, rising to his feet.

"Maybe another time," she whispered. "The kiss, that is, not wringing necks."

"Get everbody together," Crip instructed. "It's time we be heading to the house, anyway."

After an exhausting day in the field, the children went to bed early without a quibble, and shortly thereafter, Ms. Ambrose followed.

With pen and paper in hand, Rebecca sat at the kitchen table, an open book before her, and out of the corner of her eye, she watched Crip pace restlessly in the hallway.

"You going to wear your legs out," she warned, careful to keep her voice low. "You better be getting some rest while you can. We got a hard day ahead of us tomorrow, and them rows of corn don't get no shorter."

He strode to her, and placing his finger across her lips for silence, he whispered, "Come with me."

Outside, he softly closed the door behind him, and taking her by the hand, he ran from the yard, pulling her along.

"Where we going?" she whispered loudly.

"Come on," he coaxed.

"Miz Ambrose will have a cow!"

"She's asleep!" he assured her. "She ain't gonna know nothing!"

The sounds of night seemed surreal . . . frogs croaking, crickets chirping, and the hoot of an owl overhead . . . yet combined with the beating of her own heart, it set the stage for excitement.

She let him lead her to the creek bank where he promptly dropped to the ground to remove his shoes. "Wanna go swimming?"

"No . . ." she answered doubtfully.

"The last one in . . ." he dared, all the while pulling his shirt over his head.

He jumped in the water with a splash, and hesitating only a second, she unbuttoned her dress and let it fall at her feet.

Knee-deep in the water, Rebecca shivered. "Ooh-ooh! I didn't know it would be so cold at night!"

"It ain't cold over here where I'm at," he teased. "Why don't you come over here and see?"

"Why don't I just take your word for it," she laughed.

He moved through the water with ease, and taking her hands in his, he pulled her deeper in murky current. Playfully, he swam circles around her, and all at once, he ducked under the water and disappeared.

Laughing, she called out to him. "Crip?"

He didn't resurface right away, and she slapped her hand in the water, her giggles floating in the night air. "Crip?"

Overhead, a cloud inched its way between the moon and earth, darkening the night, and suddenly frightened, she looked frantically across the water. "Crip!"

Beneath the ripples, she felt him wrap his arms around her legs, lifting her in the air. Angrily, she splashed water at him and squirmed out of his grasp.

He tried to take her in his arms, laughing heartily, but she eluded his attempts and scrambled up the creek bank.

"You shouldn't do things like that!" she scolded. "What if something really happened to you? It's already scary enough out here without you acting up!"

From the water, he watched her slip her dress over her head, the moonlight silhouetting sensual appeal, and his eyes shone with appreciation.

"You shore a purty girl," he drawled.

"Yeah? Well, you a crazy boy!" she fussed playfully. "Done lost all your good sense coming out here like this."

"If that makes me crazy, then it don't say much for you, does it?" he asked, casually stepping from the water and slipping into his pants. "After all, you followed me."

She dropped to the ground beside him, combing her fingers through her hair. "The way I remember it, I don't think I had much choice."

Even in the darkness, she could see the flash in his eyes. "Didn't have a choice?" he asked, his voice unusually harsh. "You had a choice! Ever road . . . ever turn . . . ever act you do . . . you got a choice. Even if it ain't nothing but a given."

His tone took her by surprise. "What's the difference atween a choice and a given choice?"

"A big difference," he said, taking a deep breath, his voice calm now. In sketchy detail, he tried to explain. "When you see two things you like, but you can only pick one . . . you got a choice of which one you want the most. But, when it's two bad things . . . well, you still getting two things to pick from, but you don't *want* neither one, so that really ain't no choice, is it? It's a given. Like, take this place, for instance. I didn't wanna come here and I shore didn't wanna stay where I was, so picking atween the two . . . either one was a given. But, sometimes it all works out. If I hadn't come here, I wouldn't never had a chance to cut my eye at you."

"And, wouldn't that a been a terrible shame!" she smiled.

"Yeah, it would. Knowing you is something I wouldn't have missed for the world."

"Me neither," she sighed happily. "It's like it was meant to be."

"Destiny," he said, rising to his feet. "It's called destiny. We best be getting back, now. Don't want that scag waking up and finding us gone."

"But, you say she wouldn't wake up!" she scolded.

"And, you believe that? Girl, you shore are gullible."

"What's that mean . . . gullible?"

"It means you got more looks than brains."

"I got all the brains I need, thank you!" she retorted. "And, as for looks . . ."

"Like I say," he grinned sideways, bumping her shoulder, "you shore a purty girl."

All too soon, they reached the house, and quietly, they slipped inside, tiptoeing hand in hand down the corridor to her room. He lingered in the hallway outside her bedroom door, and for a moment, neither spoke.

From the darkness, he whispered her name. "Rebecca?"

He stood so close she could feel him breathing, her own breath caught in her throat.

"Rebecca . . ."

"Goodnight, Crip," she whispered.

"Yeah," he sighed heavily. "Goodnight."

A familiar wagon pulled up to the barn, and Rebecca peered from the window, puzzling over his visit.

Jesse waved to her, and wiping her hands on a worn apron, she went to meet him.

"Miss Rebecca," he nodded.

"Jesse Blevins," she responded. "What can we do for you?"

"Well, I got to thinking about that young horse and all, and I got this here old saddle that I ain't got no use for, and I thought, maybe, the younguns might want it," he rambled. "That is, if you don't think it's out of line . . ."

"Why no, it ain't out of line. That's a right charitable thing you did, bringing it here and all."

"Ain't no problem," he said, dropping the saddle to the ground. "How's everthing going around here?"

"We doing right well," she nodded, looking to the garden where Crip chopped away at a string of rambling vines threatening to overtake a thriving bed of collard shoots. "Got our first mess of green beans put in jars, and the corn's done good this year. We orta be alright come next winter."

"If you ever find yourself in need, just send word. I do anything to help out," he said, his eyes soft and caring. "All you got to do is ask."

"We much obliged for the offer. I'll be shore to keep that in mind, but I think we'll be good. Is there anything else I can do for you before you go?"

"I guess that's it, then."

"Well, thank you for the saddle," she smiled, offering her hand.

Bashfully, he removed his hat and ran his fingers through his hair. "Miss Rebecca, I . . . I hope you don't take offence, but I don't know how to say it except to come right out with it," he stammered. "I'd like to come calling sometime . . . if it sets well with you. If need be, I can speak to Miz Ambrose . . ."

Stunned, Rebecca looked to the garden and waved to Crip. He waved back, and dropping his hoe to the ground, he tromped his way through the long stretch of weeds.

Confounded, Jesse looked from Rebecca to Crip. "Less you got something for that boy?" he wondered aloud.

Her cheeks burning, she averted her eyes.

"It wouldn't be no good, Rebecca," he said softly. "A life like that wouldn't be no kind of life. That boy ain't got a row to hoe. He ain't got nothing to give you, nothing but heartache. Be like a dirt road to nowhere, a hard road to travel."

She squirmed under his gaze.

"If I be out of line, say it. You seem like a good girl and I ain't quit thinking about you since I seen you last, but if you got other notions, you can set me straight right now. That boy . . ." he shook his head, "you can do better'n that."

Her eyes flashed, and straightaway, she came to Crip's defense. "You got no cause to say that!"

"Maybe not. I poligize if I spoke out of turn."

Crip approached them, and Jesse readily accepted the outstretched hand. Clearing his throat, he excused himself. "I see you plenty busy. I be getting on down the road now."

As he rode away, Crip put his arm around Rebecca's shoulder. "What was that all about? Look purty grim from where I stand. He ain't talking about taking Midnight Star, is he?"

"Did you see his shoes?" she asked, looking over her shoulder after Jesse.

Crip frowned. "Can't say I took notice."

"It wouldn't the same ones he wore the last time! He's got two pair!"

Crip looked up as Jesse disappeared around the bend, and unimpressed, he shrugged. "So what if he does? A man can't wear but one pair at a time. You show me a man that can wear two pair, and I show you a mule."

She pondered the thought. "Yeah, I guess you right about that," she said agreeably, and shooing the chickens from the porch, she went back to her chores.

Evening settled in, and as the day wound to a close, Rebecca put the children to bed while Crip sat outside on the porch, his mind preoccupied. When the silence of night indicated all had fallen asleep, Rebecca went to the door and softly called to him. He motioned her outside, and quietly, she went to join him.

"Let's go," he said, taking her hand.

"I ain't getting in that cold water again," she whispered loudly.

"We won't. I just want to talk a minute."

Leisurely, they strolled the grounds, his arm around her shoulders, hers around his waist, and laying her head on his arm, she asked, "What is it you want to talk about?"

"Anything," he said. "Anything . . . everthing, and nothing. I just want to be alone with you, that's all. Ain't nothing wrong with that, is it?"

"No," she smiled. "I like the times when we alone, just you and me and nothing else."

"That's the times I like best, too. Just ain't enough of em."

In the black of night, stars sparkled as diamonds across the horizon, and dreamily, she cooed, "Look up there, Crip. Ain't it purty?"

"Yeah, it's purty," he agreed. "Even purtier with you standing under it."

While they watched the sky, a burning glow of brilliance shot across the atmosphere, and Crip whispered, "Look! Make a wish afore it goes away."

"Ain't no need to," she sighed. "Wishing ain't getting, but you know, if I *could* have one wish and anything I ask would be mine, do you know what I'd ask for?"

"Asides me?" he teased.

"I already got you, don't I?"

"Yeah, you do. Heart, mind and soul. What else could you ask for?"

"Well . . . I'd ask to always feel like I feel right now . . . this minute. If I could stop the world, here and now, I wouldn't never ask for nothing more'n this . . . stars to light the way, your hand in mine, and heaven waiting yonder."

"Rebecca?"

"Hmm?"

"You know what I'd ask for? Right here and now with the stars shining in your eyes and heaven waiting yonder?"

"What?" she murmured.

"I wouldn't ask for nothing . . . not one thing. Well, nothing except maybe a kiss."

She laughed. "That don't seem too far-fetched."

"Well, what do you think about it?"

"A kiss?"

"Yeah."

He held his breath while he waited for her answer, his request as unexpected as the breathless response that followed. "Ok. But, not here."

"Where then?"

"On the porch. Like in the stories you been reading to me."

"A real kiss . . . just like in the stories?"

"A real kiss."

He wet his lips, his heart beating so hard he was sure that she could hear it. Anticipation mounted with every step, and when the porch loomed in front of them, she went to the edge and leaned her back against the rails.

His palms perspiring, he took his time, and leaning in, he lightly brushed his lips across her eyes . . . her cheeks . . . her neck, tasting her as he would sample a new dish. He felt her catch her breath, and slowly . . . deliberately, he let his tongue trail across her cheek to her lips, and when she opened her mouth, waves of elation convulsed through his veins, unleashing the animal within. Losing all control, he kissed her passionately, deeply, devouring her, and from the depths of his soul, he groaned aloud, a muffled rumble of tortured pleasure. With both hands, he gripped her buttocks, and roughly, he pulled her against him, his thoughts of nothing but to have her . . . to claim her . . . *to know her*. He wanted her more than anything he had ever wanted before, and senseless with desire, he lifted her dress and thrust his hand beneath the cotton fibers.

Breathless, she tried to pull away. "I should go in, now . . ." she whispered.

"No . . . no . . ." he murmured between kisses. "Don't go yet . . ."

"Crip . . ." she gasped, kissing him back. "If I don't go in now, I . . . I don't think I can . . ."

"I want you so bad! Tell me you want me . . ."

"I do want you! But, not now," she whispered, gently pushing at him. "Not now."

He drew her back in his arms again, his lips persistent and persuasive. "You don't know how hard it's been all these months, Angel, me trying to do good by you! You got no thoughts what you do to me . . . how much I need you! It's tearing me up inside . . ."

"I feel it, too . . . maybe more! But, we got to wait!"

"Seems I been waiting all my life for one thing or another'n . . . don't make me wait for you, too, Angel!"

"Please let me go, Crip. We ain't thinking clear . . ."

He knew that she was right, and summoning his last shred of willpower, he took a deep breath and roughly pushed her away.

"Crip?"

"Go on, now," he gestured her inside, his voice hurt and frustrated. "Go on! I be there in a minute."

"You ok?"

"Yeah," he nodded, not looking at her.

"You shore?"

"I be alright. Get on in the house."

Her footsteps heavy, she paused at the door. "Crip?"

"Hmm?"

"That kiss? That wouldn't no chicken peck, was it?"

In the darkness, he shook his head, both amused and torn by her innocence. "Goodnight, Angel."

Unable to close her eyes, she lay awake hours thinking about him. He couldn't sleep either, the thin walls offering little privacy, and she could hear the bedsprings squeaking in the room next to hers as he tossed and turned throughout the night. It was well after midnight before she fell asleep.

The events of the night had taken them to new heights, to a place so overwhelming, they would never again settle for anything less. Their love had been declared, their future determined, and with the igniting of passion, they would soon leave their adolescent innocence behind forever.

Crip saddled Midnight Star, and the children rushed to the barn, eagerly awaiting the chance to prove themselves deserving rodeo candidates. While they argued over who would get the first ride, Rebecca and Crip kept supervision, and after several rounds of elimination, a winner was declared.

Butch stepped forward, no longer content to sit on the sidelines to watch, but first in line to take charge. Rebecca felt that Crip was solely responsible for the child's progress, and it stirred her to tears the way the boy had developed from a broken-spirited lad to an adventuresome twelve-year-old. He bubbled with self-confidence and character, and although he was still undersized for his age, he continued to thrive each day. Today, sitting astride Midnight Star, he tossed his cap into the air, whooping as a cowpoke on the range, and laughing, she waved to him, rallying him on.

When all the children had taken turns, Rebecca went inside to start supper. Ms. Ambrose pulled a dusty jug from under the cabinet, and uneasily, Rebecca watched her fill a stein with moonshine. She knew the old woman drank the stuff occasionally, mostly for medicinal purposes, but she had never done so in front of the children. Puzzled, Rebecca kept a close account the actions of their custodian.

All through supper, the old woman continued to drink, and when the meal was finished and dishes put away, she stumbled to the back door and yelled for Big Bruce.

Warily, Bruce entered the kitchen, but upon spotting the jug, he licked his lips and grinned. Turning the bottle bottoms up, he gulped the rank liquid until his eyes bulged and his face turned red.

"Pass that stuff back over here! Grab yourself a chair and get us some music going!"

He did as she asked, straddling a ladder-back chair, and pulling a harmonica from the bib of his overalls, he practiced a few notes before breaking into a euphonious melody. Ms. Ambrose filled her cup again, tapping her hands on the pitcher and stomping her foot to the rhythm of the music.

Dumbfounded, the children stood with their backs to the wall, and she motioned to them. "Come on, younguns! Dance!" she yelled. "Get on the floor and shake a leg. Show old Ambrose what you got!"

They made no offer to follow her instruction, and unsteadily, she rose from her chair, pulling Teddy to the middle of the floor. Laughing foolishly, she twirled him around.

"Dance, little boy! Dance til your shoes fall off!"

In the spotlight, Teddy stepped out of his shoes and skipped across the floor, while Ms. Ambrose took another swig, holding her sides as she roared with laughter.

Uncertain, the others watched, but the laughter seemed inviting, and one by one, they rose for the occasion. For over an hour, they danced around the room, prancing, swaying, and laughing, and tired at last, they dropped to the floor at Big Bruce's feet.

Bruce nodded to Crip, and switching to a melancholy medley, he played a soft serenade, a song of love unfulfilled, of wasted time, and heartache.

"Dance with me?" Crip whispered over Rebecca's shoulder.

"I can't," she declined, peering to Ms. Ambrose.

"Come on," he persuaded. "It'll give me a chance to hold you right under her nose, and she won't know the difference."

It seemed awkward at first, going round and round and round in the middle of the room with Ms. Ambrose only a few feet away, but the sounds coming from the harmonica were hypnotic, and Rebecca began to relax. She felt his arms tighten around her, and she closed her eyes and laid her head on his shoulder.

Having nodded off, Ms. Ambrose's head jerked up, and she reached for the ewer and emptied it in her cup. "Enough of that sob stuff!" she barked. "Pick it up!"

Big Bruce followed her instruction, filling the room with sounds of a lively tune, and the children took turns showing off, frolicking across the floor, their giggles filling the air.

Amidst the joyful revelry, Rebecca and Crip slipped to the porch unnoticed. Once they were out of earshot, she laughed, "I ain't never seen the younguns carry on so. Did you see Teddy? I never knowed he could move like that! They shore seem happy tonight."

"Yeah, it seems. And, you?"

"Why, it don't take much for me, Crip Chaney. Not much at all. I can be happy anywhere, long as you there."

He yearned to take her in his arms, but he knew that one kiss would not satisfy him. Instead, he reached for her hand and placed it over his heart.

"These past days I been thinking serious on getting us out of here," he said. "You eighteen now, same as me, and ain't nobody can make you stay here no more."

Her heart raced. "When are you thinking on going?"

He sighed heavily. "That's the part I ain't figured out yet. It takes money, and money's the one thing I ain't got. I been studying on hitting the farmhouses around here and see if I can't pick up a little work on the side. What with the way times are, I know they couldn't pay much, but I'd save ever dime of it. It might take a while . . ."

"How long?"

"Depends on the pay . . . a few months, I guess," he told her. "Just long enough to get us to Kingsport, or maybe Johnson City. They got jobs there . . . real jobs, not just nickel and dime trades. How do you feel about it? Are you ready?"

"I'm ready . . . been ready. I ain't never been a mile in no direction from this piece of dirt, but I'd leave here tonight if you asked me, money or not. Crip, I'm ready to start my life with you . . . whether it's across country or just up the road, makes no difference to me. I'm tired of living like this . . . tired of being denied my wants, and tired of denying yours. I'm ready for us to be man and wife."

"No more ready than me. But, we can't yet. I wouldn't never take you away from here til it's a sure thing I can give you something better than what you be leaving behind. It's a hard life out there with no money and vittles, and I ain't forgot a hour of it. But, you hold tight, Angel. It won't be long, now."

"I'll be counting the days," she whispered.

"Party's over!" Ms. Ambrose bellowed through the doorway, her eyes suspicious. "And that means all of you! Get these lights out and hit the hay! Morning comes early, and I ain't going to have you laurel up all day!"

"Goodnight," Rebecca mouthed the words.

"Goodnight, Sweet Angel."

Morning did come early, and Ms. Ambrose held her aching head. She screamed at Rebecca for rattling pots and pans and sent the children outside before breakfast. Without question, they quietly went about their chores.

In the front yard, Midnight Star nibbled at the stubble of grass beneath his feet, and moseying to the porch, he neighed loudly, rousing the fury of Ms. Ambrose.

She rushed outside, her face contorted with hatred, her lips curled in a twisted sneer, and grabbing a broom, she whacked the animal across the back.

"Shoo!" she yelled, swiping him across the back again. "Get away from here! Get your mangy ass back to the barn!"

Stomping and snorting, Midnight Star reared up, and frightened for her safety, Ms. Ambrose backed away. When the horse quieted down and turned to go, infuriated, Ms. Ambrose ran behind him, bringing the broom down hard across his back again.

At the sound of the commotion, the children came running, and as Midnight Star galloped off, Butch came from the back yard, the horse and child rounding the corner of the house at the same time. Already spooked, Midnight Star reared up again, and he came down with deadly force, his hoof landing behind Butch's ear. There was blood everywhere, and Butch lay still.

His eyes wide with the horror before him, Crip went to the child, and while Rebecca summoned the children together, Ms. Ambrose waited on the porch, the weapon still in her hand and a crazed look on her face.

His face that of a madman, Crip started for Ms. Ambrose, his fists clenching. "He's dead!" he cried. "You done kilt him!"

"You seen it!" she shouted defensively. "The horse did it! It was an accident!"

"You kilt him, you old bitch . . . you . . ."

"Oh, God!" Rebecca screamed, kneeling beside Butch and weeping uncontrollably. "Just hush! Everbody, just stop it! This baby ain't never had no peace, and now, he's laying here dead . . . can't you just shut up and give him that?"

Crip put his arms around her, and she clung to him, sobbing. Together, they carried the body inside, and gently, they laid him on the table, his small corpse a depiction of life unfulfilled, of life cheated, and of wretchedness. Rebecca paused to push his hair from his forehead, thinking how peaceful he looked, so at rest, and if not for the pool of blood beneath his head mingling with the salty drops running down her face, one might think he was only sleeping. But, he was not asleep. He had withdrawn, once more, to his lonely, empty shell.

Rebecca removed a sheet from her bed, and crying softly, she spread the coverlet over him, lightly kissing his forehead before pulling the linen over his face.

With a promise of a quick return, Bruce set out to fetch the sheriff. Ms. Ambrose shut herself in her room, and all afternoon, the children sat circled around the table. Crip sat next to Rebecca, his face hard and grim, and except for whimpers and sobs, the room was quiet. Time dragged by, the two hour round trip to Lando Ferry feeling more like days, each minute a decade.

Sheriff Neeley arrived with the mortician, and as they came through the front door, Crip slipped out the back, unnoticed.

Ms. Ambrose came out of her room, her lips clamped tight, her eyes bloodshot, her manner insolent. While the child was prepared for burial, Neeley gathered details about the incident. He took notice how the children huddled around Rebecca, and he wondered why they had latched onto the lass at a time like this instead of their caretaker. He voiced his concerns to the undertaker, making a mental note to check up on the old woman's credibility.

Based on the information given, much to Rebecca's dismay, it was determined an accidental incident.

They laid Butch to rest along with the other poor souls that never made it out of Sweet Haven. Rebecca hoped that, maybe now, he would find peace among the angels.

After that, the children clung to her as if she was the very air they breathed.

A week passed since the accident and the house was filled with mourning. Each day, the children refused to play, and every night, they went to bed with tears in their eyes and fear in their hearts.

In an effort to comfort them, Rebecca and Crip had pushed their own feelings aside. Tonight, they sat quietly watching the clock, and when Ms. Ambrose finally stumbled to her room, they slipped out the door and found their way to the creek.

Overhead, a full moon and a scattering of stars lit up the night, but on the banks of the creek, sorrow and grief clouded the air. Talk usually came easy, but tonight, words eluded them.

Crip stood at the edge of the water, deep in thought, and from out of nowhere, he asked, "Do you love me, Rebecca?"

"You know I do," came a soft reply.

He spoke with great effort, his voice ragged. "How much?" he asked. "How much do you love me?"

"You my heart," she averred. "I love you more'n life itself."

"Life?" he sighed. "Life ain't but a breath."

There was something about him, something in his manner, and alarmed, she questioned, "What is it, Crip?"

He swallowed hard, his voice quivering. "The day is short . . . and tomorrow ain't a promise."

"What's wrong, baby? Why, you shaking all over!"

As if possessed, he took her in his arms, kissing her, his lips greedy, demanding, and urgent. "I want you!" he whispered tersely. "I want you now!"

She offered no resistance, her mouth open and inviting, heightening his pleasure until all sense of reasoning dissipated and wanton need raged through his veins. His loins ached to have her, every fiber of his body demanding release, and he tore through her undergarments, his fingers combing through a mass of curls to cradle the soft mound below her navel.

She placed a trembling hand upon his. "Crip?"

"Please!" he moaned. "Please . . . I want you so bad I hurt!"

"I'm afraid . . ."

"Don't be!" he whispered huskily. "Let me touch you, Angel . . . let me make you want me . . ."

With gentle coaxing, he mumbled words of love in her ear, his kisses warm, his fingers caressing her with painstaking strokes. "Please . . . Rebecca, honey . . . I got to! I can't stop!"

"It's ok!" she murmured feverishly, caught up in his excitement. "I don't want you to stop!"

She helped him with the buttons on her blouse, and when she stood naked before him, he stepped back, taking her in.

She was even more beautiful than he had imagined, and overcome with desire, he swept her in his arms, pulling her with him to the ground. Driven by love, inflamed by lust, he unleashed secrets he had only envisioned in his dreams, and with concentrated purpose, his hands roamed her body, his fingers searching out the fleshy furrow where he slipped inside to find her relenting, wet, and ready.

He was gentle . . . more gentle than any boy without experience had a right to be. He eased between her thighs, and together, they let love carry them to a place where there was no right or wrong, to a place where nothing else mattered, until, in one rapturous moment, they fell limp and tangled in each other's arms.

Later, she was ashamed, and covering her face with her hands, she cried.

Concerned, he wiped away her tears. "I hurt you?"

Unable to look at him, she shook her head.

"You love me still?" he asked.

She nodded, tears streaming down her face. "I love you too much!" she sobbed on his shoulder.

"No more'n I love you," he said, cradling her in his arms. "Don't cry, Sweet Angel. We ain't done nothing wrong. Now, you belong to me."

"Yes! Yes, I belong to you!"

And, for the next three months, they slipped off to the creek to be alone as often as they could get away.

On a chilly Thursday morning in mid-October, a loud knock sounded at the door. Rebecca peeped through the window, and spotting the sheriff, she went to get Ms. Ambrose.

In the kitchen, Sheriff Neeley removed his hat, and Ms. Ambrose pointed to a chair. Rebecca set a cup of coffee in front of him, and he nodded gratefully before sitting down.

"Looks like we in for some bad weather," he said, noisily skimming the liquid from the top of the mug. "The wind's getting up and there's a certain nip in the air. A bad storm brewing, for shore."

"You can skip the pleasantries, Neeley. I'm shore you didn't come all the way out here for a cup of coffee and a weather report," Ms. Ambrose said warily. "What is it you want?"

"I see you ain't wasting my time, so I won't waste yours. You got a boy staying here by name of Ash Lee Chaney?"

Rebecca held her breath while she waited for the answer.

"What's it to you if he is?" Ms. Ambrose asked.

Their dislike for each other was apparent. "I come to ask the questions, and the quicker I get answers, the quicker I can be out of your hair. This Chaney boy been here?"

"No," Ms. Ambrose said, a blank look on her face. "We ain't never had nobody here by that name. Not that I recollect."

Rebecca shot her a surprised look, wondering why she would try to protect Crip. She recalled his first day at Sweet Haven when Ms. Ambrose had tossed his papers into the fire, and it suddenly dawned on her . . . the old woman could barely read at all, and she only knew him by his nickname.

He turned to Rebecca. "What about you, miss? You got anything to add?"

"Name don't rang a bell. This boy . . . Ash Lee, you say?" Rebecca dared to ask. "Has he done anything wrong?"

"Well, now, we not rightly shore what he's done. There's these loggers over in Pennington who come across some remains in the woods a couple weeks back, and seems it all boils down that they think it's got something to do with this here Chaney boy. There wouldn't much left to identify the man, what with the coyotes and buzzards taking meat . . . pardon my frankness . . . and ain't no telling how long he'd been out there, neither, as they say what was left wouldn't no more'n a heap of putrefied rottenness . . . sorry again, miss. It took a while to figure out who he might be, but the rusty knife they found laying next to him . . . that and them brogans, thirteen and a half, if I recall it right . . . well according to the county men, wouldn't but one

56

man matched the evidence, and having narrowed it down some, they went to talk with the missus and she put in a claim against Chaney that he kilt her old man. Word is, Chaney was headed for these parts last she seen of him, and that's what I'm doing here, just looking for answers, nothing more."

Solemnly, Rebecca listened, her face displaying no interest other than that of curiosity.

Sheriff Neeley squinted at her. "If you know anything, miss," he urged, "it would go better if you told it now."

Quickly, she averted her eyes and shook her head.

"Well, I guess if you don't know nothing then you ain't got nothing to tell," he said, pushing his chair from the table. "I be going now. Thanks for the coffee."

Rebecca walked him to the door, and nervously, she put her hand on his sleeve. "This old woman in Pennington . . . what would her name be?"

"Betty," he told her, searching for a hint of recognition in her face. "Betty Gilliam."

She shook her head again. "That name don't rang a bell, neither," she said.

As Sheriff Neeley stepped to the porch, Rebecca cautiously followed, checking the door to make sure that it closed behind her.

"You got something on your mind?" he asked.

Knowing that, soon, she would be leaving Sweet Haven, Rebecca feared for the children's safety when she was gone, and hoping to have a moment alone with the sheriff, she had followed him outside. Now, faced with the opportunity to dispel her fears, she was concerned that speaking out might only serve to make matters worse.

"Sheriff . . . I . . ."

He stepped to the end of the porch and made himself comfortable, propping one hip on the banister. "If you got something to say, girl, speak up," he said, taking a quick glance at his pocket watch.

"I . . . I got a favor I need . . ."

"Um-huh . . ." he nodded, pulling a pouch from his pocket and stuffing a wad of tobacco in his cheek. Gesturing to her, he offered her the bag. "Have some?"

"No, thank you," she mumbled, shuffling her feet.

"Suit yourself. Now what is it you need?"

"You don't know me, Sheriff," she said, keeping her voice low, "not from Adam, but I been here my whole life. I pert near raised these younguns myself, and they've come to spect me to be here to look out for em, but truth is, I be leaving soon . . ."

"You going somewhere?"

"Yes, sir, I hope to . . . and I was wondering . . . could you come by to check on my babies sometimes? I'd feel a whole lot better about going if I knowed they'd have somebody they could depend on . . . if need be."

"That be the old woman's job, ain't it . . . looking out for em, I mean?"

She swallowed hard. "If you could just . . ."

Out of the corner of her eye, Rebecca saw the window curtain move, and timidly, she dropped her head.

Neeley sighed heavily, his voice edged with helplessness. "I ain't blind, girl. I can see everthing ain't in accord, and I got my suspicions about what goes on around here, but without a firsthand account, ain't much I can do. It's a damned disgrace that the county don't look after our younguns like it should, but until somebody stirs up a stink, things ain't likely to change. Now, if you could help shed some light on the situation . . ."

The door creaked opened, and Ms. Ambrose stepped outside. "You still here, Sheriff? If *you* ain't got more important things to do than stand around talking all day, Rebecca has. Maybe you orta think about spending that spare time in nabbing you a killer."

Neeley ignored the woman, and turning to Rebecca, he put his hand on her shoulder. "I stop by again soon," he said reassuringly. "If you get wind of that Chaney boy, send Bruce to fetch me. And, thanks again for the coffee."

Rebecca rushed inside, and throughout the day, she avoided Ms. Ambrose. Anxiously, she waited for Crip to show, and at the first opportunity, she ran to the barn, calling his name, but Crip was not there.

Listlessly, she went about her chores, shunning the children, as she had no answers for them. They played quietly, their minds preoccupied by the unexplained circumstances of the day.

Clouds gathered overhead and a storm swept through, pouring at times, and Rebecca paced the floor. When dusk settled in, she grabbed her jacket and ran out the door.

"I'm going to check on Midnight Star," she called over her shoulder.

She ran through the forest as fast as she could, the rain blinding her, and when she reached the creek, she found him waiting in the darkness. Her body limp with fear and relief, she went to him and fell in his arms.

"My sweet angel!" he whispered, squeezing her so tightly she could hardly breathe.

She shivered uncontrollably, the lump in her throat making it hard to speak. "You alright? They come looking for you!"

"I know . . . I seen him when he come up! I waited in the trees til he left, but I was scared to come back to the house, thinking he might come back any minute! I knowed you'd come here to find me!".

"What are you going to do?"

The words tore from him like that of trapped animal. "I got to leave! Already, I should be gone, but I couldn't go without telling you!"

"No!" She shook her head, tears streaming down her face. "No! No!"

"I got to! Please, honey, don't cry," he pleaded. "Soon as the way is clear, I come back to get you! I love you, Rebecca, and we going to have that little house with the picket fence . . . six babies . . . everthing you want! But, right now, I got to go!"

"Take me with you!" she cried, her voice choking. "We'll go together!"

"I can't take you, Angel . . . I can't!"

"You say you'd never leave me!"

"And I meant it! But, there's stuff you don't know!"

"I know!" she sobbed. "I know you kilt that old man! But it wouldn't your fault! We can tell em . . ."

"It wouldn't help none no matter what we tell em! Don't you see? I kilt a man, and they ain't never going to listen to nothing we say now!"

"I can't bear it if you leave me here!"

He tried to make her understand. "It wouldn't be safe to take you with me . . ."

"Then don't go! If you can't take me with you . . . stay here!"

"I can't stay! You know I can't! Leaving is the only chance we got . . ."

"Don't leave me, Crip! Please, don't leave me!"

He locked his arms around her, his voice torn with emotion. "You know I can't go if you don't say it, but if I stay here, they going to lock me up. Is that what you want?"

She clung to him, weeping. "If you go, I won't never see you again!"

"Oh, Sweet Angel, don't you know? I got you in my heart, and there ain't nothing short of dying could keep me away! I come back! You got to believe that!"

"You come back?" she choked. "You swear it?"

"I swear it! I come back! Ain't a God in heaven if I lie!"

In her heart, she knew there was no other way. Whether he left on his own or if they came and took him away, she knew it mattered not, for either way, he would be gone, and without him, she would cease to be.

"Then go," she said, her voice drained of all emotion. "Go, and I wait for you to come."

"You wait for me here?"

She nodded. "I wait forever!"

One last kiss, and he was gone.

She stood a moment after he left, her face wet from the torrent of rain and tears streaming down her face, and racing back to Sweet Haven, she burst through the door, her clothes drenched and her heart heavy. They looked to her, and without a word, she went to bed.

A month went by without a word from Crip, and each day, Rebecca kept her eyes open, looking for the least little thing that would indicate he had come back. She walked to the creek every morning, and again at noon, and each night before she went to bed, she went again.

In Rebecca's heart, life *had* ceased to be, as she knew it would, but life at Sweet Haven had changed. After talking with Rebecca, Neeley turned his full attention to investigating the orphanage, and uncovering evidence of poor management and mistreatment of the children, Ms. Ambrose was dismissed. At the children's insistence, Big Bruce had been allowed to remain as groundskeeper.

By the decision of the county, the facility was assigned to Mr. and Mrs. Ward, a married couple who loved children but were unable to have their own. They were kind folk, educated and proper, and without further delay, began teaching the children to read and write. Taking special care with the little ones, Mrs. Ward even allowed them to call her Mommy, if they wanted.

She worried about Rebecca . . . crying in her sleep every night, rising every morning with sickness, pale and haggard, unable to eat. She kept a protective hand resting on her stomach and refused to discuss the matter.

Jesse had started stopping by unannounced. He came to discuss next year's crops, to check on Midnight Star, and to bring supplies, always inquiring about Rebecca's well-being. After a word from Mrs. Ward, Mr. Ward invited him to Sunday dinner.

One cold evening in late December, Mrs. Ward came to Rebecca. "Let's talk," she said.

Distancing themselves from the rest of the family, they went to the porch. The brisk wind tore through Rebecca's jacket, and she shivered violently.

"Honey," Mrs. Ward said, draping her arm around the young woman's shoulders. "I don't pretend to know everything that went on before I came here, but I can see that you are not well. You are in a bad situation, and it is not something that you can deny for very long."

At her words, Rebecca pulled away.

Hesitantly, Mrs. Ward continued, "The children have said . . . there was a boy? I hear you were close?"

She paused, and when Rebecca offered no response, Mrs. Ward continued. "Now, dear, this boy . . . I've heard things. Sheriff Neeley says . . ."

"The sheriff just knows the half of it! Crip ain't to blame for what happened! It wouldn't his fault . . ."

"That's what they all say, but dear, he's run away, and that alone makes him look guilty. Running off like that is not the actions of an innocent man. An innocent man would want to set the record right with the law."

"That's easy for you . . . and them like you! You don't know what he put up with, the meanness, the heartless things done to him! You never knowed him . . ."

"You're right, I never knew him. I don't know anything about him except what the sheriff has told me. But, it doesn't matter what I think about him. My concern lies with you, dear, and what he has done to you. He has abandoned you . . ."

"He's coming back! He loves me!"

"If he loved you, wouldn't he be here at a time when you need him most? Honey, you just made a mistake . . ."

"Loving Crip ain't no mistake!" she said defiantly, wiping away her tears with the back of her hand. "He's the only good thing that ever happened to me! And, it ain't like you say! He does love me! He don't know about the baby! And, he'll be back! Soon as he can, he'll come to get me!"

Mrs. Ward shook her head, her voice oozing with sympathy. "I don't think so."

"He will . . ." she said again, willing it to be so.

Mrs. Ward spoke softly, her words carrying convincing weight. "No, dear, he won't. Now, Jesse has an interest in you . . . he has indicated as much to Mr. Ward. He is a good man, and as far as looks go, he's very easy on the eyes. He has a farm not far from here. He will be a good provider . . ."

"But, I don't love Jesse!"

"You have to do what is best for you and your child, and unfortunately, love has nothing to do with it."

"Love has everthing to do with it, else what's the use? Crip loves me, and I love him!"

"My dear girl, you're so young, naïve, and trusting . . . good qualities to be sure, but not always the best in judgment. You have put everything in this boy . . . your hopes, dreams . . . you've idolized him, made him your knight in shining armor, and under the circumstances, I can relate. It is only natural that you would mistake those feelings for love. I'm sure if you had known from the beginning the things that he stood accused, you would not have allowed yourself to become entangled in this . . . this web of confusion. What you are feeling is no more than a schoolgirl crush . . . an infatuation. It certainly is not love. How could you love a boy like that?"

Rebecca spun around, tears streaming down her face, her voice breaking, *"How could I not?"*

Tears glistened in Mrs. Ward's eyes, and she took Rebecca in her arms.

"What am I going to do?" Rebecca asked plaintively.

"I can't tell you what to do. But, you have been given the opportunity to make a decent life for your child," she answered compassionately. "Don't be so quick to throw that away. Soon . . . very soon, you are going to have to make a decision. Mr. Ward has promised to give Jesse your answer by the end of the week. Think it over carefully. It isn't often that a tarnished girl gets a second chance."

Rebecca turned away. *Tarnished!* This is what their love had come to?

Mrs. Ward paused in the doorway. "Just give it some consideration. It is your choice."

But, it was not her choice! It was a given, and Rebecca already knew what her answer would be.

Year of 1909

January was the beginning of a new year and a new life for Jesse and Rebecca. They kept the ceremony simple, the soft-spoken vows barely audible, and only the Wards and children were present.

Rebecca remained stoic, forcing a wan smile each time Jesse looked her way. He watched her with concern, her face pale, her hands icy cold, and her body shook each time he tried to touch her. It was not the trembling of a nervous bride, but as whitecaps surging from the sea to claim her, washing over her, wave upon wave.

Mr. Ward pronounced them man and wife, and Mrs. Ward squeezed her hand. "You make a beautiful bride, Mrs. Blevins!" she said.

"Like a angel!" Gracie told her.

Tears sprang to Rebecca's eyes, and Mrs. Ward quickly looked to Jesse. Smiling apologetically, she explained, "Tears of joy. Every woman has them."

She pulled Rebecca aside. "You have married a fine man and he will make you a good husband. You could do worse than Jesse."

Numbly, Rebecca nodded.

One small bag held all Rebecca's belongings, and Jesse threw it in the back of the buckboard. He helped her aboard, and with a slap of the reins, they rode away. With shouts of goodbye, the children waved, and she turned to watch them until they were out of sight.

Jesse's farmhouse was small and neatly kept, the furnishing handmade and covered with rich red oak stain. She browsed around the rooms, commenting on his handiwork, shying away from the bedroom.

"It's yourn," he said simply. "Everthing I got is yourn."

The sun dipped below the horizon, and when shadows fell across the window, Rebecca looked outside, her heart sinking.

Jesse understood. "You got to be wore out," he told her. "You take the bed, and I sleep out here tonight."

Gratefully, she nodded.

Jesse spent a restless night on the settee, and barely past daybreak, he awakened to the mouth-watering aroma of coffee, hot biscuits and scrambled eggs. Rousing from the couch, he came to the table, a big smile on his face. Things were going to be all right.

But, he slept on the settee again that night, and for a week, Rebecca went to bed early, softly closing the door between herself and the man she had married.

She knew that it could not go on like this. Jesse was her husband, and she could not put him off forever.

Jesse had been patient with her, soft spoken and generous, and Rebecca wanted to show her appreciation. She asked him about the foods he liked and had spent the day preparing his favorite meal.

"You a good cook," he told her. "Everthing taste good."

Shyly, she accepted the compliment, and pushing her chair from the table, she reached for his plate.

Without looking up, he placed his hand on hers. "I'll help you," he said.

With the dishes put away, she headed for the bedroom, and without further encouragement, Jesse followed.

It was a rushed act of need for him and an act of gratitude for her. She closed her eyes, her mind wandering back to the steamy nights at the creek, how her heart had pounded in her ears when *he* touched her, and she longed for *him*. She thought about *his* face . . . *his* hands . . . *his* lips . . . and sweet passion . . . passion so intense it lifted them high into the heavens, until at last, they lay spent in each other's arms like the calm after a rampant storm! She moaned with longing, and thought about *him!*

When it was over, she wept.

Understanding and apologetic, Jesse held her in his arms until she slept.

Jesse brought in wood for the fireplace, and his smile broadened at Rebecca hanging pictures above the mantle. He nodded his approval, and dropping the logs to the hearth, he helped her down from the chair. He put his arms around her, his hands resting on her round stomach. He was pleased they were having a baby so soon, and he swore it must be twins.

Rebecca patted his hand before easing out of his arms. She had settled in her new surroundings without much ado, and taking pride in her home, had rearranged the furniture and hung bold, colorful curtains to contrast against the plain white walls. Throughout the rooms, crocheted doilies dressed up tables in country elegance, and she placed simple trinkets all about, adding her own personal touch.

On one end of the fireboard, a faded book of poetry lay . . . always in sight . . . and every time she warmed her hands in front of the fire, she reached out to touch it.

She practiced cooking with different foods, preparing tasty meals to appease her husband's appetite, and after supper, she read aloud to him.

But, she never read him poetry, or made him apple pies.

Year of 1911

An impatient knock sounded at the door, and Rebecca found Big Bruce standing in the bright sunlight, a crumpled piece of paper in his hand. Without greeting, he shoved it at her and quickly made his departure.

Her heart fluttered when she glanced at the familiar writing, and dropping it inside her pocket, she forced her attention to the toddler clutching at her skirt.

"Who was that?" asked Jesse, peeping out the window.

Rebecca wouldn't meet his eyes. "Big Bruce. Miz Ward is needing my help this evening. Could you set with the baby for a spell?"

"Yeah," he told her. "I can do that. How long?"

"Couple hours, I guess, maybe more."

She rushed to finish her housework, and at noontime, she fixed a tray of sandwiches, fried bologna and biscuits, her eyes on the clock on the wall. The minutes dragged by like hours, and at one o'clock sharp, she headed for the door.

"Want me to take you?" Jesse offered. "That mile ain't got no shorter, and it wouldn't take a minute to gear up the buckboard."

"Ain't no need!" she answered quickly. "I take the short cut through the woods. I be back soon."

The short cut through the woods was a trodden path where the children pounded the ground with their many trips to visit Rebecca. She welcomed them with cakes and sweetened juices, and they adored little Ashley, spoiling her with gifts and love. At fourteen, Michael had grown into a beautiful teenager and often begged to baby-sit while Rebecca helped in the fields.

Once the farmhouse was out of sight, she broke into a run, and leaving the well-beaten trail, she followed the creek bank to their old meeting place.

He was there! She clutched at her heart, her breath caught in her throat.

Feeling her presence, he spun around, and as if the past two years were not between them, they rushed into each other's arms.

"You here!" she uttered through kisses and tears of joy. "You come back!"

"I say I would! My God, Becca, look at you! A full-growed woman!"

"I missed you so much . . . ever day . . . thinking I never see you again! And, now you here!"

"Oh, Sweet Angel!" he whispered. "I missed you, too!"

"I keep a eye out! For three whole months, I come looking, just praying you be here!"

"I shoulda never left you," he said ruefully. "The past two and a half years has been hell, and I counted off ever day of it. There ain't been a thought cross my mind that didn't have you in it, wondering if you was ok . . . what you was doing."

"Them first months, I barely got through the days without going crazy, not knowing where you was or . . ." she choked, "if you was alive! Sometimes, I almost convinced myself that you and me was never real . . . that you was just somebody I made up, and that none of it never really happened."

Tenderly, he touched her cheek. "It happened. You and me . . . the way we felt about each other . . . it was real as rain. And, ain't nothing changed . . . nothing but . . ." he paused, already knowing the truth, but praying she would say it was a lie. "I hear you a married woman, now."

Dropping her eyes, she nodded. "Jesse. I married Jesse. You?"

He shook his head. "Won't never be but one angel for me."

Her eyes clouded. "Why didn't you come back like you say?"

"I sent word I was coming," he said. "And word come back it was already too late."

"When, Crip? When did you send word?"

"January . . . February . . . just a few months. Can't give you no exact dates, but I sent word," he averred. He didn't want to ask, but he needed to know. "How is it . . . being married to him?"

She shrugged. "I got the things I need."

"And you happy with that? You can get the things you need anywhere. What about the things you want, Angel? Do you got what you want?"

"Wants? Wants is baby talk. It's the needs that count, and wants don't matter so much, no more."

"They still matter to me, which brings me to what I come for." He dropped to one knee and took her hand in his. "I love you, Rebecca, always have and always will. That night I left, I told you I was coming back for you, and here I am, keeping my promise. And, I spect you to keep yours. Remember? You say you belong to me, and I come here today to claim what's mine. I come to take you home."

She bit her lip to hold back the tears. "That promise was made a long time ago, and we ain't younguns no more. It ain't just you and me . . . there's others to think about! I got a husband now! I got a baby, and one coming . . ."

"You got a baby?" he asked, incredulously. Somehow, although he knew she was a married woman, he had not thought of her giving herself to another man.

"A little girl! Ashley!"

Searching her face, he questioned, "Ash-Lee?"

She knelt beside him, her face glowing. "You got a little girl, Crip!" she said.

He was floored. "We got a baby? We got a baby? Now, you got to say you come with me! We a family!"

"But, it ain't a family she knows. She don't know nothing but Jesse, and she loves him so much! You should see them together! He worships her! It would kill him if I took her from him. Me and you . . . it's too late."

"What kind of talk is that? It ain't never too late to right a wrong. I was wrong to leave you that night, and you was wrong to marry a man you don't love."

"I *do* love Jesse," she said timidly, rising to her feet and turning away. "He's a good man, and . . ."

"The same as me?"

He held his breath, afraid of her answer, but when she turned around, her face told him everything he needed to know. She would *never* love another the way she loved him.

"Come with me, Becca!" he pleaded.

"You know there ain't nothing I want more!" she cried. "But, it wouldn't be right to just up and go like that!"

"It ain't right that we be apart neither. I come here today to make things right . . ."

"How? We can't change what's already been done! We made our choices, and now, there ain't nothing left but to live by em!"

"Can you live by em?" he asked. "Cause I can't. Living without you ain't no kind of living. I think about you ever minute of ever day. Ever town I go, I see you, and everthing I do, you a part of it. Can you say it ain't same for you? You don't think about me none no more?"

"Oh, my darling!" she cried. "All the time!"

"Then, come with me!"

"You don't know what you ask! I can't do it!"

"The girl I knowed could do anything if she want it bad enough."

Her eyes brimmed with tears. "That girl ain't here no more. Comes a time when you have to put away the ways of a youngun and take a long hard look at what is. We made mistakes, and *this* is what we got for it, and we can't change it no matter how bad we wish it undone."

"Everybody makes mistakes, but just cause you do, don't mean you have to keep on making em. I wish to God I'd never left you . . . but

I did, and it was the biggest mistake I ever made or ever will. But, that's one mistake I ain't making again. This time, I ain't going without you."

"You got to! Jesse . . . he's been good to me and Ashley! I can't just act like everthing he's done means nothing! And, what about the baby? I can't take a baby away from all she knows!"

"Babies forget, and it wouldn't be long til she won't remember nothing about this life. She'll come to know other things . . . to know *me!* We'll make a home together, the three of us . . ."

"And the one I carry?"

He swallowed hard. "We'll work it out, Rebecca . . . just give us a chance!"

She closed her eyes, and sadly, she shook head. "I can't do it," she said. "I love you, Crip Chaney, but I can't go with you."

"Then what am I spose to do with the rest of my life?" he choked. "I love you too much to stop now. I couldn't stop if I wanted to."

"Me neither! I'll never stop loving you!"

She fell into his open arms, yielding to his lips, this man whom she had given her innocence, her heart, her love. She wanted so desperately to tell him that she would go with him . . . that she would follow him to the ends of the earth . . . that nothing else mattered and nothing had changed.

But, it had changed!

"You best go, now," she said weakly.

"Is there nothing I can say to make you come with me?"

She couldn't bear to see the pain in his eyes, and unable to look at him, she shook her head.

He squatted to the ground, staring in the distance, his face crushed. "My baby?" he questioned. "Can I see her?"

She suppressed a cry.

"Then, I get *nothing!*"

Tears streamed down her face. "You got my heart! And, the love we feel, it's still ours! It's here," she put her hand to her chest, "and nobody can take it away . . . nobody . . . less we let em! I hold you in here til the day I die!"

Swiftly, he rose to his feet and went to her. "I can't leave you, Rebecca . . ." he moaned. "Not this time!"

"What choice do we have?"

"Walk away," he whispered. "Walk away with me and don't look back."

"I can't, Crip!"

"You mean you won't."

"I mean I can't!" she sobbed, her face buried in his chest.

Helplessly, he tried to comfort her, his mind muddled. Grasping at the slightest thread of hope, he tried to salvage a way to keep correlation between them. "Rebecca . . ." he said softly, placing his hand under her chin and lifting her face to his, "if I have to go without you . . . I will . . . but please don't send me away with nothing. Just tell me that we still have a chance . . . no matter how slim . . ."

A sob caught in her throat. "I don't see none!"

All the energy seemed to drain from him, and his arms fell lifelessly to his side. "Then I guess that says everthing, don't it?"

Through tears, she watched him walk away, and pitifully, she cried out to him, "It didn't have to be this way! You say you was coming back!"

Her words stung as though she had slapped him, and his shoulders stiffened. He didn't turn around, wanting to wound her as she had hurt him, his voice choking with emotion. "And you say you would wait forever."

He disappeared among the trees without looking back, and she fought the urge to run after him. Tears spilled down her face, and she sank to the ground, sobbing. It was almost dark when she stood up and made her way home.

Jesse never asked why it took so long for her to come home . . . or why her eyes were swollen as if she had been crying . . . or why, when Michael came to visit that very afternoon, she had not seen her and knew nothing about Mrs. Ward's need of her.

He just put his arms around her, quietly comforting her, and said nothing.

Rebecca had thought she would never hear from Crip again, and when a letter arrived in her mailbox, she rushed to the bedroom and tore it open.

"As most always, you right again," he wrote. "You got a good life now, and I don't need to be trying to root back in and mess it up. It be for the best if you forget we ever was. Just know one thing, I still love you. I'll never stop."

She answered, her words ringing with hope. "I can't forget us! I don't want to forget! Don't give up on me, my darling! Somehow, we'll find a way to make it work."

And an answer, "I ain't never been one for giving up. If I give up on you, I give up on me. You that little piece that makes me whole. You all I got."

She wrote to tell him that she lost the baby she was carrying, but she didn't write that the doctor had said her heart was too weak to carry another. She didn't write about the farm or her life with Jesse, how much she relied on the man she had married, or of the fulfillment she found in her husband's kindness and dependability, as much fulfillment as a woman can without the man she truly loves. She didn't tell him how seeing her husband and her child together almost made her own sacrifice worthwhile . . . how their adoration of each other brought joy to her heart, or that she thanked God every day for sending him to her and rescuing them from a life of disgrace.

No, she never spoke of Jesse at all. It would not be fair to either of them.

What she did write about was her undying love for him. She wrote with fevered confessions, pouring out her heart, as she knew he would not betray her confidence. Speaking freely, she expressed how much she missed him, her ardent longing for him, and her desire to see him again.

Crip letters were short; he was ok, he missed her, and he loved her. He had done well for himself; his loyalty and willingness to work had landed him a job with the railroad, the benefits including a decent paycheck and travel. Sometimes, he spoke of his whereabouts, wishing she could have been with him to see the Grand Canyon in Arizona, the snowcaps in Colorado, the Ryman House in Nashville, and Niagara Falls.

What he didn't write about was how the house with the picket fence was no consolation for the emptiness in his heart, or how lonely he felt when he lay awake at night with only her memory to hold while another man held her in his arms. He didn't tell her how every time he tried to love another woman, it was *her* face he saw, or how sometimes when he was alone, he cried.

He never told her that.

Rebecca wrote of Ashley, how she grew more like him every day, even looking like him.

"She's a handful, and I keep a close eye on her," she wrote. "She's got purpose and strength, and when I look at her, I see you. Sometimes, when I hold her in my arms, I feel like I'm holding you."

And he answered, "Ever night, I go to sleep with you in my dreams, and ever morning, I wake up with you in my eyes. You are with me, always, close as the beat of my own heart."

Each one always ended the same, "Tell my baby I love her, and when you ready . . . I come!"

Year of 1913

Big Bruce stood on the porch, and Rebecca rushed to answer the door. She knew what these visits meant. Crip was coming!

Her heart fluttered in her throat. One word!

Calling to her daughter, she went to the bureau and hid the piece of treasure in the bottom drawer. "Come Ashley! Quick! Let Mommy fix you up real purty, now!"

"Where we going?" the child asked.

"I'm taking you to Sweet Haven. You wanna go play with the other children, don't you?"

The four year old nodded.

She pulled the bonnet over her daughter's unruly curls and went to the mirror to freshen her own face. Taking the pins from her hair, she draped the tresses across her shoulders, and with the tip of her finger, smoothed a tint of color across her lips and cheeks.

Ashley couldn't keep up with her mother's pace, and Rebecca stopped several times to wait for her, rushing her along. The youngster was full of questions, and she answered absently, her mind on the note she left behind. One word!

One perfect, powerful, wonderful, blissful word!

Waiting!

Running down the path, Michael rushed to meet them, and for a moment, Rebecca drifted back to a time when she was sixteen, a time of innocence, a time of awakening, and a time of desire.

"She wants to play with the children. I won't be long," Rebecca promised.

As soon as Michael was out of sight, Rebecca took a quick look over her shoulder and made a dash through the woods. She started to run, eager to see him.

Crip stepped from behind a tree, startling her. "You come!" he breathed a sigh of relief. "I wouldn't shore if you would."

Her lips covered his, and when she kissed him, he knew without a doubt that, in her heart, she was still his sweet angel. They sat on the ground beneath the same tree where they had sat, seemingly, a lifetime ago, when she was still innocent and he had not gone away.

They talked ceaselessly . . . he . . . then she . . . then both at the same time, catching up on everything they had missed.

"Crip, is it safe for you to come here? You never really told me what happen when you left that night. They ain't still looking for you, are they?"

He shook his head. "No, I got that business took care of. When I did it . . . you know, when I kilt him . . . well, Miz Betty, she's the one who told me to go. She got the papers ready, and that's how I got here. She say to go, that she'd take care of it long as she could. The way I hear it, it took em about three years to find him, and when they got hot on her tail about it, she got scared and told em I did it. And, that's when the sheriff come looking for me and I had to leave. It was the hardest thing I ever did, leaving you. I run for about two months, and I couldn't take being away from you no more, and I got to figuring that the quicker I go ahead and get this mess took care of, the quicker I could come back for you."

She touched his cheek. "I never knowed nothing about that."

"Yeah, I know that now, but I didn't know it then."

"What happened when you got to Pennington?"

"First thing I did was go looking for Miz Betty. I figured if we went together, we could get this thing fixed up, but when I got there, she wouldn't at her old place. It took everthing I had in me, but I drag myself down to see the sheriff, and I ask him about Miz Betty. He say, didn't I know? Miz Betty dead. I told em who I was and they say they ain't looking for me no more. Afore she died, she told em she the one who done the killing and that I was free to go. I can't tell you how good that made me feel. I wanted to come and get you right then and there, but knowing if I come back broke, we'd just be stuck at the Home again, I took a job in Jonesville. That's where I was working at when I run into one of them boys from Bowen's Supply. He was making his rounds picking up provisions for the store, and I recognized him right off. I told him to let you know I would be there soon as I had the money, but the next week when he come in, he said wouldn't no need to bother. He wouldn't tell me no more'n that, and I give it a lot of thought to whaling it out of him, but not wanting to get in no trouble, I decided to come and see for myself. I lit out like all hell broke loose . . . why it couldn't have been more'n four months all total . . . but when I got to Sweet Haven, I was turned away at the door. Some man, I guess it was Mr. Ward, told me you don't live there no more and that I need to be getting on down the road and not come back. But, I couldn't do that. So, I waited a few days, and then I come back again, and this time, Miz Ward let me in. We talked about two hours, and she say you was happy and that if I cared about you . . ."

"Miz Ward?"

"Yeah. She say you done married a good man and I need to leave you be."

"Miz Ward?"

"Yeah, Miz Ward. She didn't tell me nothing about you going to have a baby, and not knowing that, I couldn't figure out no reason you would up and marry another man less you wanted to. Course, if I had knowed your take on it, a dozen mules couldn't have drug me away, but I didn't know, and believing she was right about you being happy and all, I done like she ask. Anyways, I didn't have nothing to offer you, and Miz Ward said you was all settled in over at Blevins place and doing right well. That's when I made up my mind to go to work for the railroad, thinking maybe the travel would help with forgetting you. But, it didn't. Life without you ain't worth salt, so the more I think about it, the more I knowed I had to come back to see for myself if you was done with me. I didn't want to come back empty-handed, so I waited til I had some money saved up. I wanted to show you that I could give you all the things he could . . . that and more . . . and well, you know the rest. I waited too late."

"I'm so sorry . . . so sorry," she said pitifully. "Things was so bad when you left . . . the waiting, hoping . . . just dying inside, not knowing what to do, me with child and all. Ever day, I come down to this spot right here looking for you . . . *ever day* . . . even the day I got married. It breaks my heart all over again to know that if I had just waited a little longer . . ."

He took her hand in his. "Ain't your fault things turned out like they did. Ain't really mine, neither, but it don't matter now whose fault it is. Fingering the blame ain't gonna change the outcome. I give up all claims on you that night when I left, but it makes me sick to my belly to know that I let you go for nothing."

She touched his sleeve. "You didn't have no choice."

Ruefully, he placed his fingers against his temples, squeezing hard to shut out the past. "I had a choice," he sighed.

The sun danced through the trees, and realizing how late it had gotten, she jumped up.

He reached for her hand, a piteous look on his face. "Don't go . . ."

"I got to. Come," she said, pulling him to his feet. "I got something I wanna show you."

A group of children played in the open yard, their squeals of laughter bringing back bittersweet memories.

"Which one?" he asked.

Rebecca pointed. "Can't you tell? She's just like you!"

He watched the four-year-old running around the yard taking complete charge of the others, and he smiled, his heart in his eyes. "She'll go far in life," he said. "Cause she's like you, too."

"That's Michael over there keeping an eye on em. Reminds me when I was her age. She's talking about getting married come next spring."

"Michael? She's just a kid."

"Not no more. She's sixteen . . . near seventeen now. And, you should see Gracie, too! She's one of the purtiest girls in these parts . . . got ever boy around at her beck and call."

"Don't even seem like the same place . . . same people," he sighed. "Ain't nothing like it was, is it?"

"Nothing but us . . . the love we got for each other. It ain't changed a bit."

He took her in his arms. "Then, the rest don't matter."

"I got to go now."

"The offer stays good. Anytime you say, I come and get you."

"I know."

He held onto her, and reluctantly, she pulled away. She looked back to him, and he waited in the shadows until he couldn't see her anymore.

Year of 1915

With the last of the pinecone ornaments in place, Rebecca draped a garland of popcorn around the freshly cut cedar, and stepping back, she surveyed her handiwork.

"It's purty!" Ashley squealed, unable to contain her excitement.

"It ain't done, yet," Rebecca told her. "We got one more."

She went to her bedroom, and searching through the stack of letters, she found a splintered ornament, an angel carved from a piece of wood. Carefully, she placed it on the tree, a million memories flooding her mind.

"What's that, Mommy? A angel?" the six-year-old asked.

"Yes, baby, it's an angel," she answered absently. "It's a special angel."

"Some ain't, are they?"

"All angels are special, but this one's more special than all the rest. She'll be yourn one day, and you got to promise me that you take real good care of her. Don't never let nothing happen to her. Keep her in a safe place, and never lose sight how important she is. Can you do that for me, Ashley?"

"Yes, Mommy."

Lovingly, Rebecca touched the cherub. "And, ever time you look at her, I want you to remember how much your daddy loves you. You *will* remember that, won't you?"

She went to the window and pulled back the curtain, the tears running down her cheek falling as silently from her chin as the snowflakes to the ground outside. It had been a while since she had seen Crip, although he was never far from her heart or her mind. She had received a Christmas card saying he would come as soon as he could, and for Rebecca, it could not be soon enough. She yearned for him, and in her heart she knew, that somewhere far away, all alone, he was thinking of her.

"Merry Christmas," she murmured.

Miles away from Lando Ferry, Crip stood on the front porch, a stack of firewood in his arms, and stomping the slush from his shoes, he went inside. He tossed a log in the fire, and while he warmed his hands in front of the open flames, he pondered the tree propped in the hallway.

All was still, the walls echoing his very thoughts, the sound of his own heartbeat pounding in his ears. It was *too* quiet. He searched through the stack of 78's, and selecting a disc from his beloved collection, he waited for the music to play before settling in front of the fire. Again, he debated the tree.

He considered moving it to the window, maybe throw a few decorations on it, but he couldn't see the purpose. It suited him just the way it was, bare and empty, a replica of his life.

He went to the window and peeped outside. The snow was coming down heavy now, the ice crystals covering the ground reminding him of Rebecca. It didn't take much. She was always on his mind. He could almost feel her arms around him . . . feel her soft skin against his . . . almost hear the sound of her sweet voice calling his name, and he ached for her. He wanted to see her . . . needed to . . . but with snowstorms coming daily and ice covering the roads, it was too far to travel from Knoxville. He would have to wait until spring.

The bottle of whiskey he opened this morning stood half-empty, and while he poured himself another glass, he studied the cypress. Maybe a little star at the top would make it tolerable.

Nah. It had lost its appeal and no longer suited him. He strode to the door and tossed it in the front yard.

Outside, a full moon spilled across the ice and snow, and he paused a moment in the brisk night air to absorb it all, a picturesque portrayal of peace on earth and good will. The tranquil scene, which should have brought harmony to his heart, only served to heighten his sense of isolation.

"Silent night, holy night," he whispered.

He coughed to clear the aching lump in his throat, and shivering, he went inside and barred the door behind him, stopping to refill his glass before settling on the plush rug in front of the fire. While shadows flickered across the room, he listened to his favorite songs, his mind in another world.

He must have dozed off, for the music had stopped playing and the room was dark. Unsteadily, he threw another log on the fire, and going to the cabinet, he emptied the bottle of whiskey. He started another record, and grabbing a blanket, curled up in front of the crackling flames.

Whirring around the house, the wind wailed, a forlorn sound, and in the nearby forest, searching for his mate, a wolf's mournful howl carried through the night air. Another reminder of Rebecca.

He raised his glass and murmured, "To you, Sweet Angel. Merry Christmas."

In the background, music played softly, inducing him to sleep, his dreams filled with springtime, sunshine, and Rebecca.

Rebecca and Crip continued to see each other every time they could slip away, and the letters came like clockwork.

"It was good to see you, my love. I miss you so much, my red-haired angel."

Rebecca sent pictures of Ashley. "This child of ours has made me happy more than I ever thought I could be. She's a part of us and all that I hold dear. She is her daddy's girl . . . good looks and all."

And a reply, "She is a purty one. Five more to go."

And another, "Five more babies? Would you be so awfully upset if all we have is one?"

And the answer, "I be ok with one or a dozen, it don't matter . . . long as we all under one roof."

"I love you, Crip. I love you forevermore."

"I love you, Sweet Angel."

Year of 1920

It was the middle of summer, and Rebecca stood against her bedroom door, her heart racing with excitement.

Crip was coming! His job was bringing him to Lando Ferry, and for two weeks, he would be stationed in town. Two whole weeks! Giddy with happiness, she laughed out loud.

She went about her daily chores, anxiously awaiting word that he had arrived. That day finally came.

At the creek, Crip paced back and forth, and when she came into view, he rushed to meet her.

Her heart pounded at the sight of him, and she leapt into his arms, candidly kissing him, her body burning for more than the taste of his lips. "I ache to have you!" she nuzzled in his ear. "I ache so bad . . ."

"Ain't no need to keep fighting it, Angel," he whispered, his lips on hers. "It ain't hurting nobody but us."

Emotions ran high, and surrendering to his touch, she let him fondle her, each stroke of his hand rousing her to the brink of madness, each beat of her heart screaming to have him. She yearned to rip off his clothes, to know him as she had known him years before, to stand naked in the bright sunlight and profess to the world her love for him, but somehow, she managed to push him away.

"Please don't . . . not here!"

Shaken, he took a deep breath. "You right," he said hoarsely. "Let's get out of here."

He led her to the edge of the forest where, parked just beyond the trees, a vehicle waited for them.

"What are we doing?" she asked.

"Come on," he coaxed, holding the door open. "Let's go for a ride."

"I can't . . ." she started.

"Can't never could do nothing," he said, his voice quiet and controlled. "But *you* can do anything you want. We can go back if you say."

Her hesitation was his answer, and he nudged her inside, then rushed to the other side and climbed in.

"Where you taking me?"

"Somewhere that I can have you all to myself."

"Crip . . ." she said hesitantly, "What we started back there . . ."

He took her hand. "Don't worry about it. If you don't want to, we won't. I ain't never done nothing to you that you didn't want, have I?"

She shook her head. "No, and I know you wouldn't. It's just . . . I *do* want to . . . you know I do, but . . ."

"Don't think about it. Whatever happens, happens. You're with me," he grinned.

He patted the spot beside him, and without hesitation, she slid across the seat. She knew that it was wrong, that she shouldn't do it, but she felt this was where she belonged. The guilt would come later, she was sure, and she would deal with it when it did, but right now, she was with the man she loved, and *nothing* was going to spoil it for her.

"Well, what do you think?" he asked, gesturing to the vehicle.

"I ain't never seen but four of these things! The sheriff, course he's got one, and some boy in town, he's got one, too . . . brung it back from college, I think. Then, there's them new folks that moved here from Dayton, and Mr. Bowen's got one he uses to make runs for the Supply House. Aside from that, ain't no more of em around these parts. How long you had it?"

"About two months now."

"My goodness, Crip, you must be rich!"

"Naw, I ain't rich," he said modestly. "A rich man's got most everthing he wants, and I'm still a long way from that."

He started the car, and nervously, she turned in her seat to look behind them. "I mustn't be gone long."

"How long?"

She shrugged.

"Two hours . . . three?"

"Maybe. But where . . ."

"You'll see. You just set back and let me take care of you."

Leisurely, they traveled down highways, side roads, and winding mountain overpasses, and Rebecca was amazed at the things she saw. She had never dreamed to go so far away from home and she found everything fascinating.

With Lando Ferry miles behind them, they crossed the state line, and on the outskirts of Kingsport, Crip pulled to a stop at a quaint country café. The music blared from inside, spilling out onto the parking lot, and she shook her head, her face panic-stricken. "I can't go in there!" she declared, pulling at her dress. "Look at me!"

"Like I say, can't never could do nothing," he said, opening her door and helping her from the car. "Anyhow, you ain't got to suit nobody but me, and you suit me just fine."

They found a table in the corner of the room, and when they were seated, he motioned for a waitress. He seemed friendly with the woman, commenting openly about her relationship with the bartender, and he laughed loudly when she whispered something in his ear.

"That rascal! I can see him trying to get away with it, too!"

"Yeah," she nodded. "That's what he thought. So, what'll you have today? I think we might still have a piece of that pie that you like so much."

"Just coffee for now, Louise."

Rebecca studied Crip, her eyes worried. He took her hand, and smiling reassuringly, gave her a comforting wink.

On the stage, a band played an instrumental tune, and Crip waved to the banjo player. The man acknowledged him with a nod, and Rebecca questioned, "You come here much?"

"Been here a time or two. Ever time I pass this way, I stop in. Ain't nothing special. If you seen one, you seen em all."

"Tell me how you spend your days, Crip. What's it like where you live?"

"Ain't much to tell. I got ten acres of land, and I about got our house finished now. Ever time I get a chance, I work on it some . . . you know, a little here, a little there . . . mostly just touch up. Most of the time, I'm on the road, and when I'm home, seems there ain't enough hours in the day to keep everthing caught up. There's always something that needs doing or needs fixing, so I stay purty busy."

"Tell me everthing!"

"That's about it. I get up ever morning, go to work ever day, and ever other week, I get to come home for a day or two, then start all over again. Sometimes . . ."

"Hey, Crip!" the banjo player called from the podium. "Who's the pretty lady you got with you?"

Crip motioned the guy over, and he sauntered to them, a broad grin on his face.

"Meet Rebecca," Crip introduced them. "And this ugly, unmannerly feller is Banks."

Rebecca nodded shyly and Banks whistled. "Rebecca in the flesh," he said. "So, you are real. I've heard so much about you that I thought this fool had to be talking out of his head. Ain't nobody can be *that* perfect, but damned if he ain't made a believer out of me."

"Pull up a chair and have a cup of coffee with us," Crip grinned proudly.

"We're about to start another set," Banks gestured to the band. "Come on up and join us."

Crip shook his head. "Not this time."

"You play?" Rebecca asked, her voice showing her surprise.

"Play?" mocked Banks. "Why, this boy can play the strings right off a banjo. Got a good voice to go with it, too. He even writes his own songs and everything." He turned to Crip. "You got to come up, now, buddy. Come on!"

Crip shot an apologetic look to Rebecca, and she nodded her encouragement. "Go on, Crip. Play something. I'd like to hear it."

Crip stepped to the stage and the crowd came alive with excitement. By the reaction of everyone in the room, it was apparent to Rebecca that he had dropped by more than a time or two. Everyone seemed to know him, and they all rallied him on.

He picked up a banjo, adjusted the microphone, and turned his full attention to Rebecca. In the sweetest voice, the words flowed from his lips, telling a story of friendship, a story of love, and of heartbreak.

> "Cast aside," he sang, "without a ray of hope
> I was a lonely man . . . with nowhere to go
> Then she took me in . . . out of the pouring rain
> She fed my hunger . . . eased my pain
> She gave me love . . . when there was none
> She gave me strength . . . and a reason to go on.
>
> Then one stormy night . . . we were torn apart
> Down by the creek . . . I broke her heart
> I left her crying . . . now I rue the day
> That I turned my back . . . and walked away
> If I just knowed then . . . what I know now
> She'd still be mine . . . I got no doubt.

She listened to the lyrics of love, a chapter from her own heart, bringing alive the joy of the afternoons at the creek when he had read to her from his book of rhymes, and the pain of the night he left. His voice choked through the final verse, bringing tears to her eyes.

"Hard choices made . . . hard lessons learned
Two hearts broke . . . two lives ruined
Now, miles apart . . . I bide my time
Til once again . . . the angel's mine
And, if I die . . . and it's too late
Then, I'll wait for her . . . at heaven's gate."

The room was quiet, and no one moved, all eyes glancing from Crip to Rebecca. Crip handed the banjo to one of the players, and all at once, the room came alive with applause.

"Another one!" they clamored.

The man shrugged, and reluctantly, Crip took the banjo from his hand.

"Let's speed things up a little this time," he said. "Don't wanna see no crying in here today."

His next song had the whole place stomping their feet in rhythm to the music, a humorous melody of a green-eyed girl who had stolen his heart and ended with, "And now she won't give it back!" He left the stage amidst laughter and cheers and rejoined Rebecca at the table.

"I can't believe you wrote a song about us," she said dreamily. "It was the purtiest sound I ever heard, even if it was the saddest."

"The saddest part being ever word is true," he told her. "Ever last word of it."

"I never knowed you could write like that, play the banger and all. What else is there I don't know?"

He shrugged. "I dunno. Do you know that I think about you all the time?"

"I had a hope you might."

"Well," he grinned, "do you know that I hug my pillow at night and pretend it's you?"

She nodded. "Same as me. What else?"

Serious now, he studied her, his eyes pained and sad. "Do you know how much I love you?"

Unashamed, she leaned across the table and kissed him. "I do," she whispered.

She settled back in her chair, and nervously, she scanned the room. The band started to play again, and Crip offered his hand. "Dance with me?"

In his arms, she swayed to the music, and closing her eyes, she leaned her head on his shoulder. "Reminds me of another time," she whispered. "Remember?"

"I remember," he whispered back. "I remember everthing about you . . . the way you feel, the way you smell . . . taste . . . the first time I had you. All I have to do is close my eyes, and you're mine again."

"Me too. Sometimes . . ." she hesitated, unsure how he would respond, "sometimes at night . . . I close my eyes and . . ."

"What?"

"I close my eyes . . . and I . . ." her voice wavered, trembling and breathless, "I pretend that . . . Jesse is you. Is that so very wrong?"

"No," he sighed softly. "No, it's not wrong. It's the only way I can."

"I love you, Crip."

"I love you, Sweet Angel."

They hadn't realized the music had stopped playing, and slightly embarrassed, they left the dance floor amidst smiles and nods. As soon as they were seated, Rebecca turned to him. "Is there a . . . toilet somewhere?" she asked under her breath. "I gotta go."

"Out the door and to the left. Want me to come with you?"

"I'll be alright," she smiled. "Be right back."

Inside the outhouse, Rebecca tried the door to the privy, and finding it locked, she turned her attention to her image in the mirror. She smoothed her hair, frowning at her pale complexion, and with brisk strokes, she rubbed at her cheeks.

A pretty woman, a blonde with heavily painted lips and dark eyes, stepped from the stall, and Rebecca nodded to her.

The woman eyed her curiously. "You're Rebecca, aren't you?"

Puzzled, Rebecca asked, "You know who I am?"

"Girl, everybody in this joint has heard about *Rebecca*," she said. "You're the first woman Crip has ever brought here, so we all figured you must be the one. He talks of nothing else. I've never seen a man so taken by a woman. He must love you an awfully lot."

"He does," Rebecca said with certainty. "And, I love him the same."

"Do you? Then, why is he always so down in the mouth, always by himself? If you love him, why aren't you with him?"

Hoping to stop the conversation before it went any further, Rebecca answered curtly, "There's reasons . . ."

But, the woman was not to be quieted. "Crip says it's obligations that stand in the way. And, he believes that it's nothing that time won't fix. But, you know, there's a funny thing about time. It has a way of running out."

"What are you trying to say?"

"Honey, I've known Crip a long time, long enough to know he's the kind of man any woman would be proud to call her own. There's not a single woman here that wouldn't walk out that door with him if he gave her half a chance. I think you should know that."

"Why are you telling me this?"

"Because it's you that Crip loves. He doesn't want anyone else. Unfortunately, he still believes in fairy-tales, and so he waits for the story's end . . . you know, the part that reads *happily ever after*. What he hasn't realized, yet, is that not every story has a happy ending."

"This one will," Rebecca assured her. "In due time."

"Like I said, a lot can happen in time. A man can only wait so long, and there is always the risk that you could lose him. Are you willing to take that chance? He's a lonely man, honey, and loneliness can eat a man up. He needs you . . . he needs *someone*."

"I hate it has to be this way, but right now . . ."

"Those obligations?" the blonde nodded kindly. "What about your obligations to him? All these years, he's done right by you . . . I know that firsthand. Don't you think it's time that you do right by him?"

Rebecca took a deep breath and looked away.

"Your heart is burdened, I can see that," the woman went on. "But, so is Crip's. Whatever is keeping the two of you apart . . . fix it. And, if you can't fix it, the kind thing to do is let him go. Hurting him like this . . . day in, day out . . . it's not right. The man has a lot of goodness in him, got a lot to offer a woman, but as long as you keep giving him hope and stringing him along, he will wait for you the rest of his life. But, it isn't right."

Rebecca had no response, knowing in her heart that the things the woman said were true.

"His happiness is in your hands," she said, "and you control the outcome. If you can't give him what he needs, let him go. At least, give him the chance to find it somewhere else. He deserves that much."

With that, she closed the door behind her, leaving Rebecca alone to ponder her advice.

The things the woman said weighed heavy on Rebecca's heart, and when she went back inside the café, she was quiet.

"Something wrong?" Crip asked.

"Tell me the truth, Crip . . . one way or the other . . . are you alright with you and me like this . . . just seeing each other when we can?"

He didn't answer right away, and when he did, he spoke in tones of a defeated man. "What if I say that it ain't alright . . . that living without you is the same thing as being dead? Would it change matters? What difference would it make if I say I can't sleep at night for hearing your voice calling out to me, and when I do sleep, I dream of you . . . that I pray to God to not let me wake up if I have to face another day without you there with me? Would any of it make a difference?"

She swallowed hard. "Why didn't you tell me? You can talk to me, Crip! You can tell me anything! I don't want to hear only the good stuff . . . I want to know everthing about you, how you feel, what you think . . . everthing! I know it's been hard on you! It's hard on me, too, and I hurt ever bit as much as you do. I ain't really got no life without you, neither. Course, there is Ashley, and she's a big comfort, but even she can't fill up this hole in my heart. Only you can do that. I walk around feeling dead inside, just as you do, and it is only when I'm dreaming that I am truly happy. Sometimes, I don't know which is real, when I'm dreaming or when I'm awake. Sometimes, I wonder if I'm losing my mind."

Wearily, he sighed. "I shouldn't have said anything. You got enough to deal with. I guess I'm just a greedy son-of-a-bitch. In many ways, I been a fortunate man, some might say well-to-do even, but sometimes, I just set back and look around at all I got, and I can't see nothing but all I ain't. None of it ain't worth a crumb without somebody to share it with. What I got ain't enough. I want it all!"

"And, someday you'll have it. It won't always be this way. Someday, we'll set on the porch together, you and me, watching the sun rise and set, listening to those records you got. And, at night, I will climb in bed aside you, fall sleep in your arms and wake up with you in mine. We going to grow old together, you taking care of me and me taking care of you. Our hair will grey, our faces wrinkle, and our steps will lose the pace, but we won't love each other none-the-less for it. Someday, it *will* happen, but right now, dreams is all we got."

Barely a whisper, he asked, "Is this a dream? You and me . . . here . . ."

"If it is," she murmured, "may God let us sleep forever."

"You know," he said, "I been waiting a long time to do this . . . to take you somewhere."

"Well, we here," she said. "Question is, what we gonna do about it?"

He moistened his lips. "What do you want to do?"

"What do *you* want?"

His heart leapt in his eyes. "You know what I want."

"Then what we doing here?"

He held his breath. "You hungry?"

"Only for you," she whispered. "I didn't come to eat."

She pushed her chair back and reached for his hand, and quietly, they slipped out the door.

They didn't talk, each fully aware where they were going and what would happen when they got there. He parked in front of Bailey's Inn, and moments later, he came back with the key. Without hesitation, she followed him inside.

Later, as she snuggled in his arms, he whispered, "Let's don't go back. Stay with me."

For a moment, she imagined what it would be like to forget the rest of the world, and for once in her life, do what was right for both of them. But, Jesse and Ashley crowded her thoughts, and she sighed, "If it was only that easy."

She was especially quiet on the ride home, and when she stepped from the car, he peered at her. "You ok?"

"I'm ok," she smiled uneasily, searching for the right way to make him understand her next words. "Crip, you know I wouldn't take nothing for what little time we have together, and even if it be wrong, I won't let myself feel bad about what we done today. I keep this day in my heart forever, but we can't let it happen again. We have to wait til we can make it right."

He had known what she would say before she opened her mouth. "I know," he nodded. "And, you right . . . again."

One kiss more, and she rushed home to her family.

The days flew by, and before Rebecca knew it, the first week had passed. Determined to salvage every available second, she sneaked away each day to spend time with Crip, already dreading the day he would leave.

At the creek, she rested with her head on his shoulder and her feet in the water, lazily reminiscing moments spent beneath the trees.

"Remember that time when Teddy said them bad words and I wanted slap him, but you laughed about it, and then I couldn't do it?"

"Yeah, I remember that," he said. "How is Teddy these days? Still trying to figure out what makes the world turn around?"

"No," she sighed sadly. "I don't think he cares what makes the world turn around no more. He's got other things weighing on his mind. Crip, I got a favor to ask you."

"What do you need? You know there ain't nothing I wouldn't do for you."

"It ain't exactly for me," she explained. "It's Teddy."

"What about Teddy?"

"I'm worried about him."

"What's he done?"

"It ain't so much what he's done as what's been done to him. He's going through a real hard time right now. You know, he got married a couple years back to one of them Ramey girls over in Gate City, and right off, they started a family, just like everbody does. She was a real purty girl, too, but right sickly, and when the baby come, there wouldn't no life in it, and two days after that, the girl passed, too. Teddy ain't been no good ever since. It's like he just give up."

"Poor Teddy. Where's he staying at now?"

"Purty much anywhere he can. He didn't have much to begin with, but he done lost everthing he did have. There's too many bad memories here and Teddy can't seem to find his way around em. Ain't nothing bad about Teddy, you know that good as me, but I don't know what road he might end up on if something don't wake him up. I was wondering if you could take him with you, you know, get him away from here, clear his mind, so to speak. Maybe he could get a job with you . . ."

"Teddy is family, Angel, and I'll do anything I can to help him, but I can tell you from my own dealings, you can't run away from heartache. It follows you wherever go. Traveling might help some, but not a whole lot. If it's there weighing on your heart when you go to bed, it'll still be there when you wake up. Teddy's got to be the one to let it go, and if *he* ain't ready for it, then it don't matter what nobody else thinks he needs."

"Will you try?"

"Shore. I hate like hell this happened to him. Where can I find him?"

"They say he's been seen at that tavern at the end of town most ever day. But, I wouldn't know about that."

"I'll find him, little mama," he assured her. "And, speaking of the younguns, I ain't heard nothing about the twins. How they doing?"

She smiled. "They just fine. Joe's studying to be a lawyer, and Bobby's teaching first grade down at the school. They doing right well, all things considering."

"Joe a lawyer? I should've knowed, smart as he was. Tell me, how's that working out . . . you know, with his st-st-stuttering?"

"Oh, you!" she said. "He don't do that no more and that was just plain mean!"

"I didn't mean it to be. I really wouldn't trying to poke fun, but sometimes, you just can't help the things that come out of your mouth."

"How about the things that go in?" she teased, pulling him to her and pushing her tongue past his lips.

"Umm," he said, wrapping his tongue around hers. "Sometimes, you can't help that, neither."

With less than forty-eight hours until Crip's departure, Jesse came in and made a startling announcement.

"Guess who I run into down at the Bowen's Supply?"

"Who?" Rebecca asked absently.

"That boy, Crip Chaney. Said he works with the railroad now, and was in town on business."

Rebecca's heart leapt in her throat, and she swallowed hard. "You seen Crip?" she managed to ask.

"Yeah. Seems like he done alright for hisself, too, traveling around the country and all. He's got one of them new motorcars and was dressed right sporty like. Shore surprised me. I never thought he had it in him."

"Is he ok?"

"You can find out for yourself. Set another plate tonight. He be here for supper."

Her face ashen, Rebecca swayed. "Crip's coming here?"

"Well, he put up a fuss about it, not wanting to intrude and all, but I told him it wouldn't no bother. Anyhow, it'd be a shame to be in town and not take the time to stop in to see an old friend."

Rebecca clinched the end of the table to steady her trembling knees, and concerned, Jesse pulled a chair from the table.

"You alright?" he asked.

She nodded. "Been feeling a little faint this morning. It'll pass shortly. Always does."

All afternoon, she wondered how she could get through the evening. What was he thinking coming here? How could he put her in this predicament? How could she hold her head up and keep a straight face, knowing the man with whom she had betrayed her husband was sitting at *his* table, eating the food that *he* grew with his own two hands? How could he? How could *she*?

At six-thirty sharp, Crip pulled in the yard, blaring the horn to announce his arrival.

Rebecca felt herself go weak, and she took deep breaths to calm her nerves, but his rap at the door sent the teacup in her hand crashing to the floor.

Jesse squatted to pick up the broken pieces, calling over his shoulder, "Door's open! Come on in! Find a seat and stay a week."

While Jesse headed for the living room, Rebecca lingered in the kitchen. He paused in the doorway to look at her. "Company's here."

"Be there in a minute," she said, hoping for a moment to collect herself. But, Jesse waited for her, and reluctantly, she untied her apron and followed him.

Straightaway, Crip came to her, and when he leaned in to hug her, she stiffened at his touch.

"I'm sorry," he whispered apologetically. "I just couldn't get out of it."

She couldn't look at him, her eyes downcast. "It's good to see you again," she mumbled coldly.

His face showed surprise, and stunned, he pulled away. "Yeah," he said. "You, too. It's been a long time."

"Would you like to set down?" she asked, motioning to a chair.

"We'd best go set on the front porch a spell," Jesse said, "and let some of this heat get out of here. Maybe a little breeze'll blow up off the creek and cool things down a bit. Been a real hot summer this year and looking like it's gonna get hotter."

Rebecca opted for the rocking chair instead of her usual place in the swing with Jesse. It didn't go unnoticed.

"So," Jesse began, a troubled frown on his face, "you been working for the railroad. We all wondered what happened to you when you just up and left like that. You like it? The work, I mean?"

"Um-hum," Crip nodded. "Yeah, I do. The money's good and the travel ain't bad. It's a purty good living."

"Where you staying at now?"

"When I ain't on the road, I got a house in Knoxville. Done all the work myself, and it still ain't all the way finished, but it's getting there."

"That's good. Me and Rebecca, we do all right here. Boards don't make a home, and it wouldn't nothing but a pile of sticks til she come. She fixed this old place up and made it what it is. I can't picture what it be like if it wouldn't for her."

"You got a nice place here," Crip nodded.

"Have you seen any of the old crowd from the orphanage yet?"

"Yeah, now that you mention it, I have," Crip said, turning to Rebecca. "Teddy'll be going with me when I leave. You can rest easy now. I think he's going to be alright."

Rebecca froze, and from the look on her face, Crip realized his mistake. Coughing nervously, he stammered, "Teddy knowed I was coming, and he asked me to let you know . . . said you'd never forgive him if he left town without a word."

Jesse looked from Crip to Rebecca and back to Crip again. "How long you railroad folks going to be in town?" he asked uneasily.

"Probably around six months or so. They all be gone by then, for shore."

"They?"

"I be leaving in a couple of days. They send me ahead of each crew to get things set up for em in the next town."

Jesse turned to his wife. "Well, I'm shore Rebecca's real sorry to hear that. Maybe you two can get together and talk about old times afore you go."

Rebecca's head jerked up. She could not sit here and allow her husband to give her permission to see him!

"No!" she answered sharply. "I mean, I don't see how that'd be possible. I be helping Miz Ward the next few days. Remember? I told you about that."

"That's too bad," Crip frowned. "I was kinda looking forward to it."

She shook her head. "No, I be too busy."

"Well, now," Jesse drawled, "I don't think Miz Ward would mind if you spent a little time with an old acquaintance, would she? I can run over there in the morning and tell her . . ."

Nervously, she jumped up. "Ashley! Come in, now! Supper's ready!" She turned to Crip. "Supper won't be fit to eat if it gets too cold."

It was the longest two hours of Rebecca's life. Ashley took to Crip as if she had known him all her life, and conversation flowed smoothly between the two men. It was only Rebecca who sat on pins and needles, avoiding the hurt glances from Crip and her husband's puzzled stares. Finally, the evening was over, and Crip stood up to leave.

Jesse shook his hand. "If you ever back in town, be shore to drop by."

"I will. Thank you for having me. It ain't often I get a home-cooked meal like that one."

Ashley offered her hand, and Crip pulled her to him, hugging her tight. "You a mighty special young lady," he told her, holding her a moment longer than he should. "You a lot like your mama when she was your age."

"Did you like my mama?" she asked bluntly.

"Yeah, I did," he smiled, making light of it. His eyes met Rebecca's, and under his breath, he mouthed, "Still do."

"Ashley," Rebecca instructed, "you go on and start getting ready for bed. I'll be in to check on you in a while."

"Goodnight sir," Ashley said, bounding from the room.

"Goodnight Ashley," Crip called. "Be a good girl and mind your mama."

"I'll see you out," Rebecca said, rushing him through the door.

Once they were on the porch, she checked behind her to make sure the door had closed, and quickly, she stepped away from the light of the window. Crip reached for her hand, and as if his touch had burned her, she jerked away.

"I *am* sorry about this," he said. "It was awkward as hell for me, too. You know I wouldn't never do nothing on purpose to make your life any harder, but I just couldn't come up with no good reason for getting out of it."

She nodded that she understood, and he tried again to take her hand.

She shot a quick look over her shoulder. "I really need to go in."

Her fingers lay lifeless in his hand. "Yeah," he sighed, "I guess you do."

"Goodnight, Crip."

"Goodnight."

Just before he stepped into his car, he looked back over his shoulder, his heart troubled. She was still standing where he left her, and spitefully, he gestured to the door. "Best get on inside, Miz Blevins. You don't want to keep your husband waiting."

Tears sprang to her eyes, and she watched him drive off in a cloud of dust.

The next morning, Crip sent for her to meet him earlier than planned. Hastily, she ran to the creek, stopping often to catch her breath.

He was leaning against the car when she got there, taking the last draw from a cigarette, and when she came into view, he tossed the stub to the ground and crushed it in the dirt.

Deliberately, he turned away from her and propped his foot on the running board.

"What's wrong?" she asked.

"I'm fixing to pull out," he told her. "I just wanted to say goodbye."

"Where you going?" she asked.

"This week, the upper end of Kentucky, next week, somewhere in Ohio."

"But, that's too far away!"

"It don't matter where it is, does it?" he asked indifferently. "If it's across town or a hundred miles, if we ain't together, it be all the same."

"But, you say you got two more days! Why you going now?"

He paused. "I had a thought you might be wanting me to go."

"No!" she cried, puzzled. "No, baby! Why you think that?"

He took a deep breath to steady his voice. "Last night, I watched Jesse, and I seen the way he is with you. He loves you, Rebecca, and I can't fault a man for that."

She turned away, knowing his words rang true.

"More'n that," he went on, "I seen *you* with him. It pains you to hurt him, and me in the picture ain't helping matters."

"You right! It does pain me to hurt him! Jesse ain't done no wrong, and it ain't right that he suffer cause of us! But, you and me, we count, too. Someday, we'll have our time . . ."

"There goes that word again," he said. "I can wait as long as it takes, long as I know what I'm waiting for . . . but *someday?* I don't know when that is. Do you?"

"Ashley . . . she's still a youngun . . ."

"She's growing up fast."

"But, she ain't growed up, yet."

"And, then?"

"Stay Crip!" she begged. "Can't we talk about it?"

"I'm tired of talking. What be going on in here," he said, placing his hand on his chest, "talking ain't going to fix. Two days from now, you still be with him and I still be leaving without you. It's best for everbody all around if I go now."

There was a resonance in his voice she had not heard before, a tone ringing of finality. Frightened, she asked, "You'll come back?"

He took a moment to answer, and sighing dismally, he answered, "Yeah, I'll be back. God help me, I can't stay away."

He pulled her close and kissed her before climbing into his car. "I send you a letter when I get set up," he promised. "Stay sweet, and I see you on my way back to Knoxville."

He sped away, and she ran along behind him, tears streaming down her face.

Carefully, Rebecca placed three blackberry pies in a picnic basket and covered them with a clean towel.

She called to Ashley, "Hurry up, now! We fixing to load up. And, don't forget your cap. That sun can get awful hot this time of year."

It was Labor Day weekend, and Rebecca rushed her family out the door. The Wards had planned an outing, and she did not want to be late.

Hanging from the trees, brightly colored flyers greeted them, and eager to get from under her mother's protective eye, Ashley wasted no time joining the other children.

Wistfully, Rebecca watched her go.

"Old ghosts?" Mrs. Ward asked softly, her tone concerned.

Forcing a smile, Rebecca nodded. Although she knew Mrs. Ward was partially responsible that she and Crip were not together, the woman had easily become her best friend. But, the memories she had of Sweet Haven were her own salvation, and she was not ready to share them with anyone.

Right away, Jesse and Mr. Ward delved into the upcoming election, a hot topic at every social event. Although on opposing sides . . . Mr. Ward a devout republican and Jesse an inbred democrat . . . they each respected the views of the other.

"What you think about old Cox's chances at being the next president?" Jesse asked.

"I wouldn't put much faith in that," Mr. Ward responded. "I don't think he's got a leg to stand on this time around. Of course, it's my opinion the republicans have the ticket backwards with Coolidge running as vice president. Harding may have clout, but Coolidge is the man for the job."

"Same with Cox. Everbody knows Franklin D's the better man, but you know how that goes."

Pulling on Rebecca's arm, Mrs. Ward led the way to the kitchen. "That's a subject for the men folk," she said, laughing. "Once you get them started, there's no turning them off. You can put your basket over there. What did you bring for dessert?"

Preoccupied, Rebecca didn't answer. She stared out the window, her mind flooding with painful memories . . . the hunger, the fear, the misery of poverty . . . and the boy who helped bring deliverance to them all.

"Rebecca?"

"Hmm?"

"The picnic basket?"

"Oh . . . um . . . blackberry," she answered, pulling a chair from the table.

"Blackberry's good. I sure hope I didn't cook those noodles too long. I don't think there's anything I hate worse than a limp noodle . . . pardon the pun!" Mrs. Ward laughed.

"What's that?" Rebecca asked absently.

"Limp noodle . . . well, never mind. There's potato salad in the icebox, beans baking in the oven, and I've been frying chicken all morning. I hope Jesse likes fried chicken."

The room was quiet, and Mrs. Ward looked worriedly at the young woman sitting at her table. "Rebecca?"

"Hmm?"

"Jesse . . . does he like fried chicken?"

"Don't everbody?" she nodded.

"Are you alright, dear? You're not very talkative today."

"I'm alright. Just got a lot on my mind, I guess."

"Things are alright with Jesse, aren't they?"

"Jesse's good," Rebecca sighed. "Jesse's always good. He ain't one to complain."

"I meant . . . between you and Jesse?"

"Me and Jesse?"

Mrs. Ward looked troubled, and Rebecca understood her concern. "We fine," she said lightly. "You can't go wrong with a man like Jesse."

"I'm glad to hear that. I've often wondered if I was hasty in persuading you to marry him, but under the circumstances, you must know that I was only thinking of you, dear."

"I know," Rebecca assured her.

Mrs. Ward dropped her head. "There's something else I never told you. Less than a month after you and Jesse married . . ."

Rebecca touched her arm. "I know what you going to say, and it's ok. I know Crip come back to get me. He told me all about it."

Mrs. Ward couldn't mask her surprise. "You've seen Crip?"

"Yeah," Rebecca sighed. "I've seen him."

"Still?"

There was a long pause. "Some . . . not nearly enough."

"Oh, my dear child! What are you going to do?"

"What can I do? I love Crip . . . always will. But, I love Jesse, too. You can't help but love him. What kind of woman does that make me?"

"In your case," Mrs. Ward told her, "the best kind. Now, let's get this lemonade outside before they start wondering what is keeping us. It sounds like they're having too much fun without us."

In the doorway, Mrs. Ward paused. "We'll never speak of this again," she promised, her lips pinched tight.

A ballgame was under full swing when the ladies came into view.

"Watch me, Mama!" called Ashley.

"Strike two!" shouted a freckled-faced boy with a catcher's mitt.

"Hey, I wouldn't ready!" she scowled.

Smiling, Rebecca mused, "She ain't never been ready for nothing in her whole life."

"Are you watching, Mama? I'm going to knock it out of the field!"

"That ain't likely," Jesse groaned, coming to stand by Rebecca. "The girl is breaking my heart. I don't know if I can watch no more of it. She's been up three times already . . . struck out all three."

"She won't miss this time."

And, she didn't. Ashley hit the ball so hard it disappeared into the trees, and forgetting all about the rules of the game, she turned to her mother, tipped her hat and bowed from the waist.

"Run, girl!" Jesse cheered, slapping his leg with his hat. Laughing, he put his arm around Rebecca. "That's *my* girl!"

Rebecca couldn't answer for the lump in her throat, her mind wandering back to another time when a young boy stood at bat, his hat in his hand, bowing from the waist.

All too soon, evening fell upon them, and it was dusk before they packed up the buckboard and headed home.

"It was a good day," Jesse yawned. "I'm glad we come."

"Yeah. Me, too."

"Tomorrow I get out there early and try to get the last of the backer in the barn."

"Um-huh."

"Need to get them taters in the cellar, too. We wouldn't make it through winter without taters."

"Yeah."

He looked to the overcast sky. "Shore hope that rain holds off a little longer."

They didn't talk anymore, their minds preoccupied with the matters at hand . . . his, the chores of tomorrow, and hers, poignant memories of yesteryear.

Labor Day was just another day, and after a meal of leftover stew, Crip grabbed the banjo and headed outside. He pulled his chair to the edge of the porch, and leaning back, propped his feet on the banister.

The sun disappeared over the mountaintop, and shortly after, the moon rose in perfect form, making its appearance with streaks of light filtering through the trees. Across the meadow, a whippoorwill sounded in the still night air, and with darkness settling in, the crickets and bullfrogs came alive, bringing back sweet memories of idling away time, falling in love, and making plans for the future.

Lightly, he plucked at the strings to tune the instrument in his hands. The old banjo had given him a source of comfort, an unexplainable consolation, and he spent many hours practicing different tunes and writing lovelorn lyrics.

Tonight, the soft lullabies offered him no relief, but a feeling of hopelessness. He stopped playing to stare across the field, Rebecca consuming his thoughts . . . what she was doing, what she was wearing, and if she was thinking of him. His whole being ached for her, and he wondered how long it would be before he felt complete again . . . or if he ever would.

He rose from his chair, and with brutal force, he strummed the chords as if possessed. Stomping across the porch, he danced with grievous energy, hitting the strings so hard, one by one, they popped, and still, he did not miss a beat. Shuffling his feet, he stepped spryly on his way to bed, and finally, weak with exhaustion, he fell across the top of the covers where he entered that special realm of peace he seldom experienced, that wonderful relaxation called sleep.

Year of 1924

It was too early in the day for company, but the door rattled impatiently, and Rebecca went to investigate. She looked over her shoulder before accepting the note delivered by the hands of Big Bruce.

Making excuses, she rushed to the creek where she found Crip waiting, just as she knew he would be, and she melted against him, struggling against her feelings to give in. Breathless, she pushed him away.

His voice quavered. "You don't need to be doing that, Angel . . . kissing me like that and then pushing me away."

Her face clouded at his words. "It ain't cause I want to! Do you know how hard it is for me to always have to be the one to stop . . . to not have you when I know I can . . . that all I have to do is say it and you're mine? It takes all I got to push you away, but I have to do it! When I come out here like this to see you, I have to know in my heart that it's *you* I'm coming for . . . not some tumble in the hay . . ."

"You know we wouldn't never be like that," he said, taking her hand in his. "And, yeah, I do know how hard it is for you. You a good woman, Rebecca . . . a strong woman, and I don't know where it comes from. God knows, if it was up to me, I'd take you in my arms and never turn you loose. But, come now, let's don't waste the day away. Dry your eyes and give me a smile big enough to carry with me when I go. You know, seems every time I see you, you got tears in your eyes."

He led her to the blanket spread across the grass, and dropping to the ground, she snuggled next to him. He always brought a blanket for her to sit on, and she smiled at his consideration.

"Are you ready to hear some good news?" he asked. "Teddy's getting married again."

"Teddy!"

"Yeah. The boy went out and found hisself a ready-made family, a young widow with three little kids. She's a good woman, and Teddy seems like he couldn't be happier. I hope it works out this time. I think it will."

"I couldn't be more happy for him!" she smiled, her eyes sparkling. "Tell him, will you?"

"Teddy knows already how you feel about him. We all do."

"Crip, thank you for everthing you done."

"Ain't no thanks needed. Teddy is family, and family sticks together in hard times. I'd do the same for any one of em."

"You got a good heart," she said, reaching for his hand and placing it to her lips. "Ain't many like you."

"Well, like I say, when it's family, you do what you can. Now, tell me, how's things at home?"

"About the same."

"And Ashley?"

"Ashley just like any other teenager and thinks she knows everthing about everthing. There's this one little boy at school that likes her, but she claims she don't like him back. I ain't too shore she's telling the truth. I watch her sometimes, and I see that daydreaming look in her eye, and I know that look all too well. She's been talking about moving to the city when she gets out of school. I hope she changes her mind on that."

"Keep her away from the boys long as you can, but if she's got her heart set on leaving, let her go," he told her. "Don't try to hold her back. Let her have a chance to know something asides this kind of life. Even a star in the sky gets tired of being in one place. Why do you think they fall down?"

She turned away to hide a smile, amused by his philosophy. "How are things with you, Crip?"

He shrugged. "Well, now, let me think about it. Since you asking me today, I would have to say things couldn't be better, me setting here with you and all. But, you ask me again tomorrow, and most likely, I tell you everthing's gone to hell. Either one would be the truth, and either one a lie. I got more'n any one man needs . . . a good job, some money saved up, and that big old empty house . . . got my belly full, and my duds ain't too bad, but there ain't a day goes by that I wouldn't trade everthing I got to go back to the way it used to be, back to when a hard day of work got you nothing but a sore back and we didn't know where our next meal was coming from . . . back to when we didn't have but *one* pair of shoes and they was full of holes. I guess when you come right down to it, bologna can fill a man's belly same as steak, and it's the little things what brings a man satisfaction . . . things like a woman's touch, a woman's love . . . a *woman*. So, how are things with me? Well, I got all these things I don't need, but I ain't got the little things. I ain't got satisfaction."

She recalled her conversation with the woman at the restaurant, and her heart was pained by her own selfishness. She had Jesse and Ashley to fill the lonely hours in the day, and all he had was handful of letters and a few stolen moments at the creek. Saddened by his loneliness, her eyes brimmed with tears.

He touched her face pityingly. "Please don't do that again. I been thinking a lot, lately, about the way things stand with you and me . . . you know, you here, and me always somewhere else. Me coming here can't be helping you and Jesse none, and it don't seem to be getting us nowhere neither."

He had opened the door, and faced with the choice to offer him a chance at a better life or clinging to him to save her own, she searched her soul for the right answer. He deserved a meaningful existence, a chance for happiness, or at the very least, a chance for some sort of normalcy. It would be the right thing to do, and she opened her mouth to tell him that he should not come back, to go in search of someone to share his dream, that it was alright and that she understood.

But, the words failed to come. She had loved him too much and for too long to let him go . . . for more than half her life, she had loved him . . . and if he wanted a second chance with someone else, he would have to be the one to say it. If he chose to move on, it would destroy her, she knew, but she vowed to herself that she would not say anything to obligate him further.

She forced the question from her lips, "Is that what you want?"

"What's that?"

"To stop coming . . . to end you and me?"

He looked away, his words hinting of uncertainty. "I ain't denying that leaving you behind ever time I come is getting old, each time harder than the one before, and there don't seem to be no end of it in sight, but while it ain't the best of situations, I don't know if I could go on not seeing you none. Probably do me in. Why? Is that what you thinking . . . that I should quit coming?"

"Only if that's what you want," she said, trying hard to keep her voice neutral. If she asked him to stay in her life, she knew that he would, but this had to be his decision and she mustn't pressure him in one direction or the other.

"Ain't but one reason I'd stop coming, and that's if you say not to . . . and don't know then if I could stop."

"Are you shore, Crip? Are you really shore?"

"That's one thing you ain't got to worry about on my end. Long as you got a heart for me, I'll be here."

Relief flooded her face. "I was afraid you was wanting to be done with me!"

"And, I had a notion you was getting ready to tell me to not come back."

"I wouldn't never tell you that! Seeing you like this is the only thing that gets me from one day to the next, and if I knowed I couldn't never see you again, I couldn't take it! I'd just die!"

"Shh, Angel," he comforted. "Don't carry on so. I'll always be here."

"I love you so much," she choked. "You my heart, Crip, the very beat of it . . . the breath I breathe! You the first thing I think of when I wake up . . . you the last thing I see before I fall asleep! I live only for your love . . . for the day when we can be together . . ."

The suffering in his voice tore at her conscience. "And, when is that day, Rebecca? Can you tell me when it's going to end, this pushing aside our wants and needs for the wants and needs of others? Ever time I leave you, I got this hurting, like my heart is rip to pieces, and sometimes I don't think I can take another day of it. How much longer we got to wait? Just tell me that, Rebecca . . . when?"

She pulled his head on her shoulder, cradling him against her. "Not too long, my darling, not too long, now . . . when Ashley grows up."

Year of 1926

Ashley turned seventeen, and Rebecca received another note. Crip was waiting. Hurriedly, she changed her dress and rushed out the door.

From the garden, Jesse called to her, startling her. "Where you off to in such a rush?"

"It's . . . it's Miz Ward," she stammered. "She's needing me again."

He pushed his hoe into the newly plowed soil, and propping on it, he watched her with concern. "You been running off a lot to help out with them orphans. I shore could use your help today. Can't you go another day?"

"I promised to . . ." she stopped, unable to come up with a legitimate excuse.

"What?" he asked, his eyes searching hers. "What is it that you got to do this time that can't be put off another day?"

"I promised . . ." she swallowed hard.

He stood quietly for a moment, his expression tugging at her heart. She almost told him that she would stay, but then, he dropped his head and said, "Run on, then. Just don't be too long."

"I won't," she promised, quickly turning away to shield him from the tears running down her face.

She took off at a brisk pace, and halfway through the woods, she grabbed her chest, the crushing weight taking her breath. With difficulty, she struggled to make it to the creek.

Alarmed, Crip ran to meet her, and she fell in his arms, trembling, clinging to him, her tears spilling down his shirt.

"What is it? What's wrong? Is Ashley . . ."

"Everthing is wrong! It's wrong what we be doing!" she sobbed on his shoulder. "It ain't spose to be like this . . . all this sneaking, the lying . . ."

Wearily, he sighed. "No, it ain't spose to be like this," he said, helping her to the blanket on the ground. "It was *me* you was spose to be with."

"I try so hard, but ever way I turn, somebody's getting hurt!" she cried despondently. "Sometimes, I think that nothing I do from now on is ever going to be enough to right all the wrong I done! I got a good man that ain't done a harm to nobody, and God knows I do my best to do right by him, but I can't put no heart in it! I do things no good woman would do . . . sneaking off to be with you, writing letters that's got more love on paper than I give my own husband at home! When I'm with you, nothing else is real, and there ain't nothing . . . *nothing* I wouldn't do just to see you . . . to keep you! I lie for your love, and I got this guilt inside, and the more I lie, the more it grows, and it's smothering me! I got a war going on in here, and I can't take no more of it!"

He wrapped her in his arms, rocking her, comforting. "Honey," he said softly, "remember the first time I come back and begged you to go away with me, and you said you wouldn't leave Jesse? It killed me that day to leave you again, but you was right. It was the best choice you had at the time, all things considering. But, that was then, and this is now. Ashley's grown, and Jesse has had his time. Now, it's time for us. You know what you have to do."

Her mind muddled, she couldn't comprehend what he was saying. "What?" she asked.

His voice was low, and she strained to hear him. "Another year and Ashley be eighteen . . ."

She nodded. "Come next July."

"It can be like it was in the beginning . . . just you and me . . . the way it should've always been."

Her mind spun out of control. "You and me?"

"Ain't that what you want? Ain't that what we both want . . . been waiting for . . . to have our turn?"

Quickly, she rose from the ground and turned away, and he followed her, his heart heavy by her silence. He put his hands on her shoulders and turned her to face him, searching her eyes for an answer. He didn't find one.

The words came hard, but this time, he was not leaving without satisfaction. "Angel," he said, his voice faltering. "You know that I love you more'n anything on the face of the earth, and I been waiting longer'n any man should've ever had to . . . for *fifteen* years, I been waiting. Now, next year, Ashley be out of school, and then there won't be no more need for you to stay here."

"Next year?"

"Next year . . . next summer when school is out. Rebecca, I got to hear you say it," he pleaded. "Tell me I ain't been waiting all these years for something that ain't never going to happen! The time is now . . . time you had a say in who you want, and time you be saying it!"

"You the one I want . . . the one I love! It was always you!"

"That ain't an answer."

"Next year! Yes, my baby, yes!" she assured him. "Next year!"

Year of 1927

Ashley stayed true to her word, moving to the city and leaving her mother behind with an empty house, four walls, and Jesse.

Rebecca lived for Crip's letters, sometimes checking the mailbox twice each day. He had written of his hopes to have her join him, and she kept those letters close to her troubled heart, unable to respond with the answer he needed to hear.

"I set by the fire, and just knowing you soon be here with me, I can't hardly stand it. I can feel you here already. I can't wait to hold you in my arms in our own house."

And she wrote, "Got a letter from Ashley. She's wanting me to come see her. She's got a little apartment . . . just two rooms, I think. But, she ain't that big, so I guess it'll do."

He wrote, "Had a dream about you and me last night. We was just kids, but we wouldn't at Sweet Haven. We was somewhere else, and you was laughing so hard. God, you looked good! I want you! When?"

And an answer, "The house is lonesome with Ashley gone, and sometimes, I find myself going through her stuff. I miss her so much. I miss you!"

"It's time, Sweet Angel. I'm waiting!"

With pen in hand, Rebecca stuffed the letter inside an envelope, the letter that would change her life forever, and taking a deep breath, she ran her tongue across the flap. She held it for a moment in her shaking hand, and closing her eyes, she sealed it shut.

"Come!" was all it read.

Crip was coming! Today, when she saw him, he would not leave her behind! Today, she was going home!

She couldn't look at Jesse and she couldn't sit still. She went to the window and looked to the newly planted maple, straightened the curtains, picked up pictures and set them right back down. She watched the clock, and Jesse watched her.

"I feel like a chicken in a chicken coop," she told him. "I'm going for a walk."

"I'll come with you," he said, reaching for his hat.

"No!" she said, a little too quickly, a little too harsh. She turned away. "I go alone."

His heart sank. He *knew* where she was going. Since that summer when Crip had come to supper, he had known where she went when she was supposed to be helping Mrs. Ward. He'd had suspicions all along, but needing to see the truth for himself, he had invited Crip to his home, and watching them together, he knew! Afraid that he would lose her if he forced her to openly acknowledge the affair, he had chosen to keep it to himself. After all, as long as Ashley was here, he was certain that the woman he loved would always return to him.

But, Ashley was not here anymore.

His voice trembled. "Rebecca . . ."

A thousand things went through his mind that he wanted to tell her . . . what a good wife she had been, how she had brought joy to his life, how he couldn't go on if anything happened to her . . . how much he worshipped the ground she walked on, adored her, loved her!

But, she knew these things already.

He swallowed hard, not daring to look at her. There were no words to make her stay. His shoulders drooped, and he simply said, "I ain't nothing without you. *Nothing!*"

And, just like that, she knew that he knew, and in spite of it, he had given unselfishly of his goodness and love.

"I'll be back," she said, but her words resounded with doubt. "Wait for me . . . here."

She could feel his eyes on her as she walked away, and she stood in the open doorway, her heart breaking, knowing that when she left this time, he would never see her again.

"I got to go!" she cried. Closing the door behind her, she ran through the forest, tears streaming down her face, and sobbing, she fell against a tree and laid her head in her arms.

Ahead of her, the man who possessed her heart, the man she longed for, the one she loved . . . waited. And, behind her, the man who adored her, cared for her and her child, the man who had made her all she was . . . waited. Her heart torn between them, she weighed her conscience, her loyalty to one, her love for the other.

She thought about how differently her life might have been *if* Crip had never gone away, *if* she had waited for him to return, or even *if* she had gone away with him the first time he came and begged her to leave. There had been choices in her life. She and Crip had made them, and Jesse had been there to atone for their decisions. He had done nothing . . . nothing but to love her and her child, giving her a comfortable home, security, and peace of mind, and reaching a decision, she rose to her feet and found her way through the forest.

Crip looked up as she approached him, his face beaming by her presence.

"I prayed for an angel," he whispered in her ear, "and she fell in my arms!"

She held onto him, squeezing him, her heart bleeding.

"This day's been a long time coming," he grinned, his eyes shining with happiness. "Are you ready?"

She covered his mouth with hers, her voice filled with tears, "Take me, Crip!" she cried. "Please . . . make love to me!"

"Here?"

"Here . . . now . . ."

"Okay . . ." he whispered. "Okay!" and running to his car, he returned with a blanket.

Her eyes lost in his, she unbuttoned her dress, and with subtle deliberation, she slipped the straps from her shoulders to expose her breasts, hesitating only a second before letting the material slip through her fingers to the ground around her feet. Her face glowing, her heart trembling, she stood nude in the midday sun and waited for him.

As magnet to steel, he came to her, kissing her all over, her mouth, her neck, her shoulders, his hand following the curve of her back. With a firm grip, he pulled her against him, groaning with desire.

"My God, Rebecca! I love you so much! Tell me it's real . . . tell me that I'm not dreaming!"

"Shh, my darling!" she whispered. "Don't say nothing! Just love me . . . love me!"

She welcomed him, his hardness pushing at the fabric in his jeans, his tongue circling her lips, the protection of his arms. Savoring every moment, she kissed him back, her tongue caressing the muscles on his chest, each rippling muscle so unlike the boyish frame she had known years ago. There was no existence but for theirs, the sound of her own heartbeat eliminating all else, and she knelt to the ground, pulling him with her. Nothing else mattered except the love between them, and she gave herself freely, making love and memories to last a lifetime. They clung to each other, until at last, satiated and drained, they lay limp in each other's arms.

"My sweet angel . . ." he whispered.

"Shh . . ."

She pulled his head to her breast, and in the shelter of her arms, he slept while silent tears streamed down her face.

It was late, and she had to go. Hastily, she dressed while he dreamed.

He awoke, and watching her, he knew what he had always known. She would never share a home with him, never sit on his porch to watch a sunset, and never fall asleep in his arms.

"Rebecca?"

She dropped beside him, and taking his face in her hands, she pressed her lips to his, silencing him. "I will *always* love you, Crip Chaney! Always!" she choked through the tears. "Don't never forget that!"

Tearing herself from his arms, she ran through the forest without looking back.

It was the last time she would see him.

Rushing through the door, she stood against the wall, her heart pounding, her face emotionless.

Jesse looked up, relief flooding his face, but watching her, he knew this was not where she wanted to be. She had returned to him, but he could take little pleasure from it, his happiness bittersweet.

"You home?" he asked anxiously.

"I am now," she answered, her body slumped, her eyes lifeless.

She went straight to the bedroom, and locking the door behind her, she didn't come out until the next morning. They never spoke of that day again.

Crip had written to her, taking all the blame for her actions.

"I know you feel bad, Sweet Angel, but don't. If I had not left you long ago, you would be with me. It is all my fault. I hold no hard feelings for you. Only love. I go to my grave with it."

She answered, "Ain't nobody's fault. You done what you had to do then, and I done what I had to do now. I want so bad to go with you . . . for it to be like it was, but we could never be happy if we had to hurt somebody else to get it back. It ain't who we are."

He wrote, "I read a poem and it made me think of you, as everthing does. It was all about loving somebody you can't be with . . . how he can feel her in his heart, and she can feel him touching her, even when they ain't near each other. I can feel you like that. Can you?"

"Always, my darling! I close my eyes and you are here with me. Wherever you are, there my heart is, also, for I give it to you long ago. I love you!"

Over the next few years, the letters continued to come, but not as often. Rebecca rose each morning with a prayer for Crip's happiness, and every night, he did the same for her. Though they had reached the end of what could have been, their passion never waned, for wrapped inside their hearts, the memories they shared kept their love alive, raging on, deeper than flesh, stronger than blood, and wider than the miles that separated them.

A love so powerful, that nothing, save death, could bring it to an end.

Year of 1931

In the front yard of a two-story house, Crip solemnly leaned against a picket fence and lit a cigarette. He studied the finished construction before him, an erection of wood and nails constituting what some would call a home, but it had never been a home to him. It was a house . . . his house . . . built with blood, sweat, and dreams . . . a house he hoped, one day, would be the home he would share with the woman he loved, a home where he would raise his children, a home where his heart belonged and not just a place where he hang his hat. He had put every stick in place, every design detailed with Rebecca in mind, for he never stopped believing that, one day, they would have a life together. His dreams for the future had not been fulfilled, still he greeted each day with fortitude, clinging to undying hope, for hope was all he had left. Now, hope too, was gone.

A visit to the doctor had confirmed his suspicions. He had tuberculosis, and his dreams of a life with Rebecca would never come true. He would never hold her in his arms again, and so he held her in his heart, for it was there that she would never leave.

With one last puff, he flipped the cigarette to the trail of gasoline leading from the porch, and he watched the flames burst into the sky before climbing into his car. He looked back one more time before driving away.

Yes, he nodded. *Rebecca would have liked this house.*

Rebecca would have made it a home.

Year of 1934

It is Jesse's birthday, and with plans to bake a chocolate cake, Rebecca heads to the henhouse. She pauses to wave to her husband in the field, and humming softly, she fills her basket with fresh eggs.

The short trip to the barn has left her exhausted, and with an overwhelming urge to rest, she eases in the porch swing. Lately, she has found herself tired and worn to a frazzle. She needs rest, but Rebecca never takes naps . . . never has time to.

She turns her attention to her husband laboring behind the plow, a man she respects more than anyone she has ever known, and her heart aches for him.

Involuntarily, she closes her eyes, the sounds from a rusty chain soothing her to relaxation, and in the brightness of a midday sun, she yawns.

She doesn't know how long she slept, but when she stirs from her nap, she finds Jesse standing over her, his face worried, his eyes afraid, the basket of eggs still at her feet.

"Are you alright?" he asked.

"I must have dozed off," she mumbled. "What time is it?"

"A little after five."

"Looks like supper is going to be late again," she sighed apologetically.

"You was talking in your sleep . . ."

"I was dreaming," she smiled. "I was a girl again . . . back at the orphanage. Teddy, the twins . . . all of em was there . . . looking just like they did back then. Hmm."

Wearily, she reached for the basket of eggs. "I'll get supper started."

"Don't worry about it," Jesse told her, his voice concerned. "If you're not feeling good, you just set here and . . ."

"I won't hear it," she groaned, trying to get to her feet. "You've been working all day, and I'll get supper on the table, same as always. It'll just be a little late, that's all."

"Are you shore you up to it?"

She nodded. "Yeah. If you'll just get the fire built, I'll take care of the rest."

"That ain't no problem, but I'd druther you just set here. It won't kill me to skip a meal."

Smiling, she placed a gentle hand on his arm. "Have I ever let my husband go to bed hungry?"

Uneasily, he watched her, then nodded. "Ok," he said quietly, his voice gentle and caring. Not once in their twenty-five years of marriage had he ever raised his voice. Strange that today, after all these years, she would take note the softness in his tone. "Soon as I get the chores out of the way, I'll be in to help."

She nodded, lingering a moment longer to watch him trudge to the barn.

While he threw down a bale of hale from the loft and filled a trough with cool water, Rebecca stood in the kitchen watching a pan of potatoes come to a boil. Remembering the letter inside her brassiere, she tore open the envelope, and with the back of her hand, stifled a cry tearing at her throat.

"My Dearest Rebecca,

I'd rather rip off my right arm than tell you this, but the doctors thought it would come easier if you heard it from me. Crip is dead. He's been purty sick for a while now . . . tuberculosis . . . and has been living in a sanatorium the past couple of years. I been mailing all his letters to you so you'd not know, as that is the way he wanted it. He never could bear to hurt you, and it kills me to be the one to do it now.

If you want to come, he was laid to rest at Grace Memorial Gardens up in Appalachia. I'm so sorry. If you ever need me, send word.

Yours faithfully,
Teddy

Crip was dead!

The boy of her youth, her childhood hero and the love of her heart was gone, departing from a world that had only brought him turmoil, heartache, and injustice.

No! Please, God, no!

"What's that?" Jesse asked.

Stunned, Rebecca looked up. "It's Crip," she whispered. "He's dead."

With mixed feelings, Jesse drew a long breath. The old familiar ache that had weighed heavily on her heart . . . and at times, his . . . was back to haunt them once more.

"I'm sorry to hear it," he said kindly. "Are you ok?"

"I will be. No need to fret," she answered numbly, her hand on her chest and eyes cast to the floor.

"Come and set down," he told her. "You ain't got to do this. There's leftovers aplenty."

She let him help her to the settee, wanting to scream at the top of her lungs, to crawl into a hole and weep tears enough to wash away the anguish ripping out her heart, but she must not break down now. Not in front of Jesse. It would not be fitting to shed tears for another man.

He went to the kitchen to finish up, and when the table was set, he called to her, "Come and eat something, Rebecca. You got to keep up your strength. Doing without ain't going to help none."

They ate in silence, and for once, Rebecca didn't mind the quietness. Her throat ached with swallowed tears, and she pushed her plate away, her food barely touched.

With supper over and the last dish put away, she went to the porch and eased in the swing next to her husband. Awkwardly, he patted her knee, his smile sympathetic.

Jesse had never been one for conversation, and although, at times, Rebecca would like to have shared her innermost thoughts, it was a minor grievance. Their years together had given her an understanding of him, and she had kept her feelings to herself . . . then, as today . . . learning to cope with her own devils alone.

The sound of a creaking swing and distant trill of a whippoorwill did little to pacify her aching heart, and she yearned for a moment of privacy . . . a moment to cry without guilt or conscience . . . . a moment to grieve.

Before the last traces of sun had settled over the horizon, Jesse stood up. "It's bedtime. You coming?"

Rebecca wanted to say she would be in after awhile, but he had never gone to bed without her, and although she hesitated, she knew that tonight would be no different. He offered his hand, and forcing a faint smile, she reached for his calloused palm and followed him inside.

Long after his even breathing told her he was asleep, she lay quietly, staring at the moon-streaked ceiling, unable to close her eyes.

Crip was dead!

Soft tears wet her pillow, and she held back sobs until she felt she couldn't breathe. Pain squeezed her chest, the sharp jabs more intense than usual, and she eased out of bed, careful not to rouse her husband. In the stillness of night, she tiptoed to the small den . . . a makeshift office for Jesse . . . and found her way to an easy chair. Looking out the window, she watched the orange moon rise over the treetops, and pulling a worn blanket around her, she prayed softly to the stars above.

Her tears fell freely now, and it seemed hours that she sat there sobbing out her heart before finally curling up and drifting into troubled sleep.

She rose early, making breakfast as she did every morning, and through the bedroom door, she called for Jesse to get up.

Yawning, he came to the kitchen where he found her leaning against the cabinet, her face wincing in pain. "You still hurting?"

She nodded, and he pulled a chair from the table and eased her into it before pouring himself a cup of coffee.

He stood with his back to her. "You had a rough night?"

"Purty bad."

"You be wanting to go, I guess . . ."

"If it's alright . . ."

"Shore. Get ready and I'll take you."

The four hour drive to Appalachia was silent, her mind in anguish, her heart banded with pain. She put her hand to her chest, and with labored breath, she closed her eyes and tried to rest.

"We here," Jesse said, gently shaking her.

She felt her knees go weak when she stepped from the car, and Jesse offered his arm to steady her. Inside Grace Memorial Gardens, Jesse looked for the custodian, and while Rebecca waited in the corridor, she felt the heaviness in her heart begin to ease.

Crip was here! He was here!

Jesse motioned for her, and they followed the caretaker to the cemetery behind the church. The sight of the newly-filled grave brought Rebecca to her knees, and she placed her hand in the soft dirt, her mind tormented with memories.

Jesse removed his hat and bowed his head for a moment in prayer. "Amen," he said, and when he turned to go, he patted Rebecca's shoulder. "I leave you alone a minute."

She didn't look up. "You a good man, Jesse," she swallowed hard. "I've always loved you for it."

He nodded, and with hat in hand, he left her alone to say goodbye.

She wondered about the choices she had made as her life flashed before her. She thought of Sweet Haven, the children, Big Bruce, even Ms. Ambrose. She thought of Butch. He would be ok, now. Crip would look out for him.

She thought about the times she spent at the creek . . . of Jesse, and Ashley.

And, she thought of Crip. She could see his face clearly now, feel his presence, hear his laugh.

Exhausted, she leaned against the monument and placed her hand upon his name, tracing the letters with her finger. Tears streamed down her face, and she leaned forward to ease the ache in her chest.

"Oh, Crip!" she sobbed.

"*Rebecca . . .*"

At the sound of his voice, her heart quickened. In the distance, she could hear Jesse calling to her, his voice faint and far away. "Come, Rebecca. It's time we go, now."

"*Yes, Rebecca,*" Crip whispered, his hand outstretched. "*It is time! Come with me, my sweet angel.*"

As a glow of warmth embraced her, the sweet sigh of death escaped her lips, and in the shelter of his arms, she placed her hand in his, and together, Rebecca and Crip walked into the heavens and never looked back.

THE END